HEIRESS
Elliott Granddau

Bridget Elliott, the granddaughter of publishing billionaire Patrick Elliott, shortly has become the subject of a nationwide police search after going missing four days ago.

Ms. Elliott, 28, was last seen in the Hamptons, where she attended her brother Cullen's wedding at The Tides, the Elliott family estate. According to a hired valet, her vehicle was seen leaving the estate at 10:12 p.m.

Police were alerted when Ms. Elliott failed to show up for work at *Charisma* magazine, part of the Elliott Publications Holdings, where she is employed as a photo editor. Residents in her SoHo apartment building have not seen the missing heiress in days.

shortly before the wedding from an unidentified caller who claimed to have information the woman wanted. At this point police do not suspect foul play.

Family patriarch Patrick Elliott told reporters that his family would spare no expense of their reported billion-dollar worth to locate Ms. Elliott. "We won't rest until she's back home, safe and sound," the soon-to-be retired CEO said. "No matter what it takes."

Dear Reader,

Things are heating up in our family dynasty series, THE ELLIOTTS, with *Heiress Beware* by Charlene Sands. Seems the rich girl has gotten herself into a load of trouble and has ended up in the arms of a sexy Montana stranger. (Well...there are worse things that could happen.)

We've got miniseries galore this month, as well. There's the third book in Maureen Child's wonderful SUMMER OF SECRETS series, *Satisfying Lonergan's Honor,* in which the hero learns a startling fifteen-year-old secret. And our high-society continuity series, SECRET LIVES OF SOCIETY WIVES, features *The Soon-To-Be-Disinherited Wife* by Jennifer Greene. Also, Emilie Rose launches a brand-new trilogy about three socialites who use their trust funds to purchase bachelors at a charity auction. TRUST FUND AFFAIRS gets kicked off right with *Paying the Playboy's Price.*

June also brings us the second title in our RICH AND RECLUSIVE series, which focuses on wealthy, mysterious men. *Forced to the Altar,* Susan Crosby's tale of a woman at the mercy of a...yes...wealthy, mysterious man, will leave you breathless. And rounding out the month is Cindy Gerard's emotional tale of a pregnant heroine who finds a knight in shining armor with *A Convenient Proposition.*

So start your summer off right with all the delectable reads from Silhouette Desire.

Happy reading!

Melissa Jeglinski

Melissa Jeglinski
Senior Editor
Silhouette Books

Please address questions and book requests to:
Silhouette Reader Service
U.S.: 3010 Walden Ave., P.O. Box 1325, Buffalo, NY 14269
Canadian: P.O. Box 609, Fort Erie, Ont. L2A 5X3

CHARLENE SANDS

Heiress Beware

Published by Silhouette Books
America's Publisher of Contemporary Romance

Special thanks to Jefferson County Deputy Sheriff Jackie Tallman for her
help and guidance in getting the facts straight. My heartfelt gratitude goes
to one-time Navarro County Deputy Sheriff Betty Swink and Hollis Swink
for their help and constant loving support. And a big thank-you to
senior editor Melissa Jeglinski for creating such a great cast of
characters for the Elliotts continuity series.
Acknowledgment
Special thanks and acknowledgment are given to Charlene Sands for
her contribution to THE ELLIOTTS miniseries.

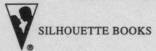 SILHOUETTE BOOKS

ISBN 0-373-76729-3

HEIRESS BEWARE

Books by Charlene Sands

Silhouette Desire

The Heart of a Cowboy #1488
Expecting the Cowboy's Baby #1522
Like Lightning #1668
Heiress Beware #1729

Harlequin Historicals

Lily Gets Her Man #554
Chase Wheeler's Woman #610
The Law and Kate Malone #646
Winning Jenna's Heart #662
The Courting of Widow Shaw #710

CHARLENE SANDS

resides in Southern California with her husband, high school sweetheart and best friend, Don. Proudly, they boast that their children, Jason and Nikki, have earned their college degrees. The "empty nesters" now have two cats that have taken over the house. Charlene's love of the American West, both present and past, stems from storytelling days with her imaginative father sparking a passion for a good story and her desire to write. When not writing, she enjoys sunny California days, Pacific beaches and sitting down with a good book.

Charlene invites you to visit her Web site at www.charlenesands.com to enter her contest, stop by for a chat, read her blog and see what's new!

THE ELLIOTTS

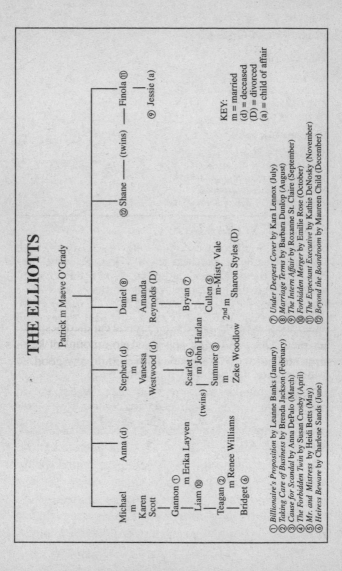

Patrick m Maeve O'Grady

Michael
m
Karen
Scott

Gannon ①
m Erika Layven

Liam ⑩

(twins)

Teagan ②
m Renee Williams

Bridget ⑥

Anna (d)

Stephen (d)
m
Vanessa
Westwood (d)

Scarlet ④
m John Harlan

Summer ③
m
Zeke Woodlow

Daniel ⑧
m
Amanda
Reynolds (D)

Bryan ⑦

Cullen ⑤
m-Misty Vale

2nd m
Sharon Styles (D)

⑫ Shane ─── (twins) ─── Finola ⑪

⑨ Jessie (a)

KEY:
m = married
(d) = deceased
(D) = divorced
(a) = child of affair

① Billionaire's Proposition by Leanne Banks (January)
② Taking Care of Business by Brenda Jackson (February)
③ Cause for Scandal by Anna DePalo (March)
④ The Forbidden Twin by Susan Crosby (April)
⑤ Mr. and Mistress by Heidi Betts (May)
⑥ Heiress Beware by Charlene Sands (June)
⑦ Under Deepest Cover by Kara Lennox (July)
⑧ Marriage Terms by Barbara Dunlop (August)
⑨ The Intern Affair by Roxanne St. Claire (September)
⑩ Forbidden Merger by Emilie Rose (October)
⑪ The Expectant Executive by Kathie DeNosky (November)
⑫ Beyond the Boardroom by Maureen Child (December)

One

"Don't you dare die on me," Bridget Elliott pleaded for all she was worth. But the darn rental car died despite her plea. The motor shut down and no amount of key turns and pumps to the gas pedal would do any good.

She peered out the windshield to view nothing but vast dry Colorado land, an abundance of road ahead and a bright dawning sun that promised a sweltering day to come. A born and bred New Yorker, she was accustomed to scorching June days, but she'd never been to Colorado, and from the look of the place, she hoped she'd never have reason to come here again.

But her mission was just, and the hot tip she'd received last night during her cousin Cullen's wedding reception had put her on a late-night plane. She'd flown all night, making plans and hoping to add one last chapter to the book that would expose secrets and lies her grandfather had imposed on their family for two generations. Patrick Elliott, the family patriarch, owner and CEO of Elliott Publication Holdings, one of the largest magazine empires in the world, would finally be exposed for the man behind the image. There'd be no more positive spin on the Elliott clan. Bridget planned to clear the air, uncover family secrets and expose scandals with truths that could knock her grandfather off his feet.

He deserved it. The last stunt he'd pulled, earlier in the year, had stunned and angered the whole family. He'd announced his impending retirement, but instead of picking his successor, he thought to make a bitter game of it, pitting his four children against one another for the job.

It had been the last straw for Bridget.

So for the past six months, she'd been searching for Aunt Finola's child. The baby, conceived when her aunt was a teenager, had been given up for adoption—an adoption forced upon her by her own father, Patrick Elliott. Bridget suspected her dear aunt had never gotten over the loss, choosing instead to devote her life to *Charisma* magazine to fill the void. Being the photo editor at *Charisma,* Bridget often witnessed the sense of loss in her aunt's eyes, even now, more than twenty years later.

And Bridget had finally made a breakthrough with, hopefully, a reliable tip from someone who claimed to know the identity of the child. She had to get to Winchester. She had to locate Aunt Fin's daughter. Finding her aunt's child would secure the ending chapter in her book. The world would finally see the kind of man her grandfather really was.

It was close to 6:00 a.m., yet not a soul appeared on the road. Of course, if she'd broken down on Highway 25, she would have been rescued by now, but the directions given by her tipster had taken her off the well-traveled road to this two-lane highway.

Bridget sighed, slumping in her seat. She didn't have time to waste. Then she remembered her cell phone. At least she could call for help, maybe get a replacement car out here quickly. She reached into her purse, coming up with the phone. But her hopes dimmed immediately. Dead battery. Heck, Bridget was forever forgetting to plug the darn thing in to recharge. That made two dead batteries in the span of a few minutes. At least, she *thought* her car's battery had died. But maybe not. Maybe it was just a fluke.

She tried the key in the ignition one more time. "Come on, please," she pleaded to the car gods. "Start, damn it."

Like an unruly child, the Honda Accord refused to comply. Nothing. Not even a little grunt of a sound. "The rental company is going to hear about this," she muttered, slinging her purse over her shoulder and exiting the car.

She slammed the door shut and began walking. Vaguely, she remembered seeing a sign a while back that Winchester County was ten miles ahead. If her calculations were correct, she'd have about a five-mile trek to reach her destination.

"I can do this," she said, her three-inch-heel boots grinding on the asphalt. Always fashion conscious, a true-blue testament for *Charisma*, Bridget now wondered why she hadn't thought to pack her walking shoes.

Where were her Nikes when she needed them?

Sheriff Macon Riggs bounded out of his patrol car and strode with purpose toward the woman lying on the side of the road, her body motionless and damn close to the edge of the cliff. She would never have survived the steep drop had she fallen. The woman faced side-ways, with her legs twisting awkwardly, but it was the blood at the back of her head that worried him the most. No doubt she'd hit that sharp wedge of granite beside her, the one smeared with blood.

As he came closer, he noted a face devoid of ex-pression, but beautiful all the same. Dark blond hair framed her face, and her lips, still pink with life, were slightly parted.

He took her hand and gave a squeeze. "Miss, can you hear me?"

Mac hadn't really expected a response, but the woman's eyes snapped open immediately. She stared up at him, blinking several times, and he gazed into amazing lavender-blue eyes. The combination of blond hair, fair skin and that particular shade of blue made the woman memorable by anyone's standards.

He leaned in closer and reassured her. "I'm Sheriff Riggs. You're going to be all right. Seems you had an accident."

"I did?" She spoke softly, with furrowed brows and a puzzled expression that suggested she was dazed from the head injury.

"Looks that way. You hit your head on a rock."

Again, she appeared confused.

"Hang on and don't move. You're close to the edge of the cliff. I'll be right back."

Within a few seconds, Mac returned to her side with the first-aid kit he kept in his patrol car. "I'm not going to move you until you give the okay. Do you feel pain anywhere?"

The woman shook her head slightly. "Not really, except my darn skull's pounding like a son of a—gun."

Mac held back a grin, admiring her attempt at restraint. "I bet. You think you can sit up?"

"I think so."

He knelt down, wrapped his arms around her shoulders and helped her to a sitting position. The material of her raspberry-pink sweater bunched up in back under his fingertips, but it was the V-neck in front that drew his attention. After one swift glance, he kept his eyes averted from soft skin and mind-blowing cleavage, focusing instead on helping the injured woman. "That's good. I can look at the back of your head now."

"Does it look bad?"

Mac did a cursory examination. The blood had clotted to her hair and there was no further oozing. No telling how long she'd been unconscious, though. It was a good thing Mac thought to patrol this road from time to time. Or she might just have rolled the wrong way, right smack into Deerlick Canyon.

"Actually, you're pretty lucky. It doesn't look too bad." Mac sat behind her, positioning himself to attend to her injury. He dabbed at the gash with moistened gauze, parting her hair to see the extent of the wound. "Does this hurt?"

"No. Keep going."

"What's your name?" he asked, to distract her from discomfort she refused to admit. He'd seen her flinch the moment he touched the gauze to her head.

"My...name?"

"Yeah, and while you're at it, want to tell me what you were doing up here? What happened? Did you fall?"

The woman tensed, her body becoming as rigid as a plank of wood.

When she still hesitated, Mac softened his tone. "Okay, first let's start with your name."

"My name is..." she began then started again. "My name is..."

She scooted away from him enough to turn around. She stared into his eyes, blinking, with a panicked look on her face. "I don't know," she said, her voice elevating. She paused again, her eyes darting in all directions, seemingly searching her memory. "I don't know who I am! I can't remember anything!"

Tears pooled in her eyes and she blinked hard, trying to keep them at bay. With desperation in her voice, she repeated frantically, "I don't know. I don't know."

Mac stood, then reached down to take both of her hands and slowly help her up. With her erratic behavior, he wanted her away from the edge of the cliff.

"It's going to be okay. We'll have the doctor check you out."

"Oh, dear God. I can't remember anything. I don't know who I am, what I'm doing here." Pleadingly, she tugged on his sleeve. "Where am I?"

"You're in Winchester County."

She stared at him blankly.

"Colorado."

She shook her head hard, her eyes wide, and Mac saw the determination on her face as she tried urgently to remember something. "Do I live here?"

"Don't know. Seems you were on foot. But we'll search for a car later. There's no sign of your belongings, either. No purse or backpack or anything. If you had anything with you, I'd guess it went over the edge when you fell down. That's *if* you fell. But I can tell you one thing for sure, with those boots you're wearing, I doubt you were hiking."

She glanced down at smooth black leather boots, then noted the rest of her apparel. Designer jeans, light-weight cashmere sweater, a black suede belt that slanted over the material and across her hips, but oddly, no jewelry other than a watch with one bright diamond on the face. She took all of this in with no recognition. It was as if she were staring down at a stranger's clothes. "I can't remember. Dear God. Not one darn thing!"

"C'mon, let's get you to Dr. Quarles." Mac took her hand, but her legs buckled when she took her first step. "Whoa," he said, catching her.

He turned her toward him, her body pressed against

his. She clung to him, wrapping her arms around his neck, leaning in for support. He held her for a minute as she rested her head on his chest. She seemed to need this moment to regain her composure, or maybe to simply lean on him for moral support. He understood her alarm. Waking up in a strange environment, with no sense of who she was or what she was doing up here, had to be frightening.

As Mac patiently held her, his own sense of composure came into play. A professional lawman, he denied the pulsing thump in his throat and the slight acceleration of his heartbeats. Yet, she was soft and beautiful and felt damn good in his arms. It had been quite a while for Mac. He'd almost forgotten what it was like to hold a woman. But her next words brought him back to task.

"My head's spinning."

Mac didn't hesitate. He lifted her up in his arms and walked slowly to the patrol car. Before setting her inside, he took a few seconds to make a mental scan of the area. No car, no sign of her belongings anywhere. Later he'd come back with a few deputies to scour the vicinity. Right now he had to get this young woman to the doctor.

And then he'd try to learn her identity and unravel the mystery of her appearance here.

She didn't know who she was. She didn't remember one thing about herself. Her mind spun and she focused her eyes solely on the man holding her in his arms. Sheriff Riggs. He held her gently, but with strength, and she felt protected and safe. She depended on the comfort he lent as she gazed into his dark eyes. He had nice eyes, she thought, and probably a good smile when he let his guard down. But she got the feeling Sheriff Riggs didn't do that all too often.

She'd been lucky he found her when he did. She'd been lucky she hadn't rolled off that ridge into the canyon. But that was where her luck ended. She searched her mind over and over during these past few minutes, hoping that something would register. Anything.

Nothing did.

The sheriff placed her in his patrol car, leaning in awkwardly, brushing her body with his. As he released her, his arm grazed just under her breasts and she silently gasped at the accidental contact.

"You okay?" he asked, his face inches from hers.

He paused a moment and stared at her, their eyes locking. She nodded, breathing in his aftershave, a subtle manly, musky scent that defined the sheriff. She got the feeling he'd protect her with his last breath if need be. Instinct told her he took his job and his life seriously.

He got into the driver's seat and started the engine. "Let me know if anything looks familiar," he said, slanting her a glance as they drove off.

Again, she nodded. She peered out the window, watching as the high ground they'd traveled became level. They'd entered a valley where cattle and horse ranches lined the highway. Mountain ridges off in the distance provided a majestic backdrop to the rest of the scenery. Again she searched her mind endlessly for any hint or clue as to her identity. Did she live here? Was this her home? Or was she on a mission of some sort? Or a vacation? Was she meeting with someone?

When nothing came to mind, she closed her eyes, willing the dizziness away. She prayed the doctor would have good news for her.

"Stay put," Sheriff Riggs said once he pulled into a driveway and parked the car in front of a small medical building. "I'll come around and get you."

"I think I can walk." She opened the car door and let herself out. Warm air hit her and she took a steadying breath, leaning on the car for support.

Sheriff Riggs was beside her instantly, looking at her with concern. "Not dizzy anymore?"

"I didn't say that," she said, feeling the effects again of standing upright. "But it's getting better."

Without hesitation, he wrapped his arm around her waist and helped her into the doctor's office.

Thirty minutes later, after Dr. Quarles had given her a full examination, he called for the sheriff. "Mac, it seems this young lady has a form of amnesia. With retrograde amnesia, the patient can't recall anything that happened before the accident or incident. A blow to the head could have caused it, but this kind of amnesia can also be brought upon by stress. The good news is that she has no permanent damage. Physically, she's fine. Oh, she'll have a headache for a day or two. Wouldn't be a bad idea to have a few tests done at the hospital to be sure, though. The injuries are minor, but I'd feel better if she—"

"When will I get my memory back?" she asked pointedly, interrupting the doctor.

Dr. Quarles shook his head, peering down at her through his glasses with kind brown eyes. "I can't answer that. Could be hours, days or weeks. Sometimes a patient goes for months without regaining his memory. Usually, with this kind of amnesia, you'll start recovering older memories first, but I have to warn you, you may never remember ones that might have caused the amnesia in the first place. The mind tends to block those out."

"Then I may never remember why this happened to me?"

"That's right. There's a chance of that," the doctor answered. "And let me know right away if those headaches don't subside. You should feel much better by tomorrow."

"But…but," she began as her situation became clear in her mind, "you're saying I'm not going to regain my memory soon?"

"Soon?"

"Today. Doctor, I need to know who I am. Today!"

"I'm afraid that might not happen. There's no way of knowing."

"Surely there's something you can do." Alarmed, she began to tremble, her body shaking uncontrollably. "No," she said, rubbing her forehead. "No, this isn't happening. Where will I go? What will I do?" She refused to cry, but couldn't control her shuddering. Panicked, she shook even more. She didn't know a soul in Winchester County. Or anywhere else, for that matter. She didn't know if she had family here. She didn't know anything about herself. She searched her mind again, trying hard to recall one memory, just one. But nothing came to mind. She didn't even know her own name! This all seemed like one horrible dream.

Dr. Quarles glanced at the sheriff before settling his gaze on her. He spoke softly, in a reassuring way that gave her reason to believe that the good doctor had met his true calling in life. "My wife and I have a spare room in our house. Used to be our daughter Katy's room, but now she's grown and married. You're welcome to stay with us until we can sort this all out."

She was at a loss. She didn't know what to say to such a generous offer. Words weren't enough to express the gratitude she felt. Her throat thick with emotion, she managed to murmur, "Thank you, thank you."

"Well then, it's settled. Let me just call my wife and let her know we're having a houseguest."

Her gaze shifted to the dark, unreadable eyes of Sheriff Riggs. For some odd reason, she needed his approval. In just a short time, she'd come to rely on the man who had most likely saved her life this morning.

The sheriff stared at her for a long moment, as if making up his mind about something. His lips quirked for an instant, not quite in a smile, but something just short of one.

"Wait up, John," Sheriff Riggs said in a commanding tone, stopping the doctor before he exited the room. "I have another idea." Then he turned his attention to her, with a dark piercing gaze. "She should stay with me."

Two

Maybe it was because he felt responsible for her safety, or maybe it was the way she looked up at him with those amazing blue eyes, but Mac couldn't abandon his "Jane Doe." Not even to John and Doris Quarles, one of the nicest couples in Winchester County.

Something inside him just couldn't do it, and the invitation fell from his lips without hesitation.

Jane stepped off the examining table to look him squarely in the eye. Her brows furrowed and she spoke in a tone that seemed...hopeful. "You want me to stay with you?"

He nodded, but added clarification. Hell, he wasn't propositioning her. If he'd met her under different circumstances, without a doubt he'd be interested. And not too many women interested him lately. But Mac was wiser and much more cynical when it came to the opposite sex now. He'd had a bad track record, a failed marriage among other things, to prove it. But something about Jane Doe struck a nerve. He'd lend her his help, food and shelter, and that would be it.

"It's strictly business. I live behind the jail and it will make my investigation into your past easier if you're close at hand. Dr. Quarles lives—" he glanced at John, hoping to get this right "—at least fifteen miles out of town. Correct?"

Dr. Quarles nodded. "That's right. Doris and I have a nice place, but I'm afraid it's outside the city limits."

Mac explained, "I live with my sister, Lizzie. You and I won't be alone, trust me. Lizzie's a schoolteacher. She's around teenagers all day long. She'll love the adult company."

"Doctor, that does make more sense," Jane explained to John Quarles. "I need to work with the sheriff to find out my identity. Thank you for the offer. Both of you have been so kind and generous to me." Jane Doe smiled, and dimples peeked out from the corners of her mouth. Mac took credit for that smile and immediately halted that train of thought. No sense getting caught up in blue eyes and a curvy body. He had a job to do. And he'd bet the woman would get her memory back real soon. Either that or someone would come looking for her.

"Are you through with your exam?" Mac asked the doctor.

"Yes, I've given her a prescription for pain, but I

want to know if there's more dizziness, fainting or anything unusual."

"You got it," Mac said. Then he faced his new house-guest. "Are you ready, Jane?"

"Jane?" She wrinkled her nose.

"Jane Doe," he said softly. Hell, he had to call her something. "Unless you prefer another name?"

"My real name would work wonders," she said a little sadly, with a slant of her head.

"I'm gonna work on that straightaway."

Again she looked at him with hopeful eyes, then shrugged a shoulder. "Jane's as good a name as any, I suppose."

"Okay, Jane. Let's get you home." And for the first time in his life, Mac was taking a woman home to meet his doting younger sister.

You'd have thought he'd been the one who'd hit his head on a rock.

"Don't let me keep you from your work, Sheriff," Jane said, sitting across from him in his cozy kitchen. He'd driven her to his house, after showing her the Winchester County Sheriff's Station, which was just yards away, up on the main street of town. His house sat on a quaint residential street just behind the jail.

While the sheriff's station could be considered contemporary, with angles and large floor-to-ceiling windows, the sheriff's home was anything but. She liked the charming three-bedroom house the minute she'd stepped inside. There was a lived-in warmth about the place.

"Call me Mac," he offered with the slightest hint of a smile. "And this *is* work. I hope you're up to a few questions. I'm going to take a drive out later today with my deputies to scour the area where you fell." Mac slid her a cup of coffee and a turkey sandwich he'd whipped up at the counter.

"Oh, thank you."

"It's my job," he said automatically.

She chuckled. The man was all business. "No, I meant for the meal."

He glanced at her for a moment, staring into her eyes. "It's hardly a meal. Lizzie's better at cooking than I am. She'll be home after three."

"I hope she doesn't mind having me here."

Without pause, he stated, "She won't. If anything, she'll talk your ear off. My sister loves a good conversation, especially if she's the one doing all the talking."

"Oh, I get it," Jane said, teasing the all-too-serious sheriff. "That's why you wanted me here. Takes a load off, does it?"

Instead of a sharp denial, he played along, much to her surprise. "You got it. You're nothing if not perceptive."

Jane drew air into her lungs. With her situation so desperate, she couldn't put much energy into being witty. "Thanks for the sandwich." She took a bite, then sipped her coffee. "What did you want to ask me?"

Mac scratched his head, then leaned forward. He paused a moment, his gaze traveling the length of her. When his eyes stopped on her chest for the briefest of seconds, Jane's breath caught. Electricity sparked in the air, filling the small kitchen. He liked what he saw, and though he had tried, he couldn't conceal that initial jolt. After all Jane had been through today, that brief instant in time brought her a definite dose of satisfaction.

Silly, of course, but true. Jane didn't know much about herself, but she understood something about the opposite sex. And Sheriff Macon Riggs, physically fit and mentally sound, was one heck of an appealing man.

"I need to know if you came up here on your own. Or if someone meant to do you harm. Sorry, but I have to ask."

The thought of someone out to harm her hadn't crossed her mind, yet she didn't feel alarmed. In truth, she felt blank, like an unused sheet of paper. Jane searched her memory, hoping for a flicker of recognition. "I don't know. I can't remember. Do you think it's possible that someone deliberately left me up on that cliff?"

"I don't know. Maybe. A jealous boyfriend? It's been known to happen, but the reality is that you've got no identification on you. I didn't see a car abandoned on the road, but we'll check that out. And you had nothing in your possession."

"I know," she said, tamping down her frustration. She knew the sheriff was only trying to get at the facts. "It's strange, but I have no answers for you. The only thing I remember is waking up on that road, with sunlight warming my body, looking into your eyes. I remember thinking you had nice eyes," she said, revealing aloud what she meant to keep to herself.

The sheriff stared at her, again with an unreadable expression. Jane shrugged off her embarrassment at that last statement, reminding herself to keep her most private thoughts to herself. She realized, though, that she might not know enough about herself to keep quiet. Each new revelation, even one as small as Mac's attractive dark eyes, meant something to her. She had so little to go on and knew so little about herself that she felt as if each new observation could be a clue to her identity.

She wondered, this time definitely keeping her thoughts to herself, if her attraction to Mac Riggs was a natural reaction borne out of his rescuing her, or if she might have automatically categorized him as "her type." She wondered if she liked the tall, dark and deadly serious kind of man, ones with strong features and sexy eyes.

"Anything else?" she asked, grabbing for the plates.

Mac immediately reached out, brushing his hand over hers, taking the plates from her. The contact startled her and she froze, her heart leaping in her chest. His touch sent shivers down her spine in a decidedly good yet unwelcome way. Jane had enough to worry about without lusting after the man who had been kind enough to take her in, offering her shelter and protection.

"I don't expect you to wait on me," he said firmly.

The breath whooshed out of her. "And I expect to pull my weight around here. Now, if you don't have any more questions, I'll clean up the kitchen. Don't you have an investigation to carry out?"

Mac blinked and his lips thinned, but Jane was certain he held back a grin. "Yes, ma'am. I'll get right on it." He snapped to, standing tall and puffing out his chest. Once again taking control. "Lizzie'll be home shortly. You need anything before then, call the jail." He scribbled a number on a notepad on the counter. Then he clapped his tan hat on his head, scowled once as she began clearing the rest of the table, and nodded in farewell.

He strode to his patrol car, which was parked on the driveway. As she watched from the doorway, she decided he was just as appealing from the back side, wearing a pair of tan pants hugging a tight butt and a chocolate-brown uniform shirt stretching across very broad shoulders. He slid into his car and started the engine, taking one last glance at her before pulling away.

Funny, with Mac around she'd felt safe and protected. But as soon as he left, her bravado failed her. She was alone. Not just in a strange house, but alone in her head. She had no memory, nothing to call upon, nothing to seek solace in, and that more than anything else frightened her.

Jane wandered from room to room, getting acquainted with a home she did not know, ready to meet a woman, who, regardless of all of Mac's assurances, might not appreciate an intruder.

Jane crossed her arms and hugged herself, warding off another case of trembles. She didn't know if she had the fortitude to survive without her memory. Right now nothing seemed real. She walked into the room Mac had designated as hers for the time being, and lay down on the bed. The full-size mattress accommodated her comfortably and she noted the cheerful surroundings. She guessed Lizzie was the decorator in the family, the whole house having female touches like lacy curtains and wall sconces with scented candles, so unlike the no-nonsense Sheriff Riggs.

Jane curled up on a soft chenille quilt and closed her eyes, as fatigue from a harrowing day caught up to her. She only hoped that when she woke up, somehow her memory would return.

And this nightmare of a day would be over.

Jane woke to the sound of humming, some catchy tune she didn't quite recognize. She opened her eyes to unfamiliar surroundings, blinking as she darted her gaze around the room. Everything seemed…off. For a second nothing registered. Then, in an instant, it all rushed back to her and she remembered her sudden appearance here in Winchester County. She remembered Sheriff Riggs taking her in. She'd fallen asleep in the guest room in his home.

Jane sat upright in bed, hoping that she'd remember something more than the past few hours of her life. When nothing jumped out at her, she rose quickly and peeked her head out the bedroom door in search of whoever was humming.

"Oh, hi! I didn't mean to wake you," announced a slender woman with short auburn hair and Mac's espresso-brown eyes. She approached, walking down the hallway wearing a big smile. "It's the song. I just can't seem to get it out of my head. I didn't realize I'd been humming and disturbing your peace all at the same time. Some songs just do that to you, you know."

"I didn't recognize it," Jane said, searching her mind for any clue. "Should I?"

"Not if you don't listen to country music. It's Tim McGraw's latest.

"Oh," Jane said with a shrug, learning something new about herself. "I guess I don't like country music."

The woman smiled once again and put out her hand. "Hi, I'm Lizzie, Mac's sister. Don't worry, a few days around here and you'll hear every doggone country tune known to man."

Jane took her hand and, instead of a shake, Lizzie placed her other hand atop hers and squeezed gently. "Mac told me all about your situation. Sorry to hear about your amnesia. That must be strange, not knowing who you are." She cast her a warm, soothing smile. "You're welcome here for as long as it takes to regain your memory. Don't tell him I said so, but Mac's the best there is. If there's a way to discover who you are, he'll find it."

Jane nodded. She had already pegged him as a dedicated lawman. "He's calling me Jane Doe."

Lizzie frowned. "Now, isn't that original. That man has no imagination."

"It's fine, really. Call me…Jane."

"Okay, Jane. Nice to meet you. And welcome. *Mi casa es su casa.*"

"I can't tell you how much I appreciate your hospitality. Your brother has been so kind. And now you. Thank you from the bottom of my heart."

Lizzie waved off her thanks with a quick gesture.

"I'm glad to have the company. Mac told you I teach at the high school. Little devils, all of them. But I love them, just the same."

Jane laughed. Lizzie had a way about her that put a smile on your face. "It's easy to see you love your job."

She nodded. "I do. But I'm ready for a break. School's out soon and I have the whole summer off."

Jane wondered about her own job status. Did she have a career? Would someone be missing her soon? Or had she traveled here on some kind of vacation? It seemed that all of her conversations reverted right back to square one. Who was she? And why was she in Winchester County?

"Tell me," she asked Lizzie curiously, "that song you can't get out of your head. What's it about?"

"'Live Like You Were Dying'? It's about living life to the fullest. About getting the most out of life while you're still here on earth." She lifted her shoulder in a little shrug. "At least, that's my interpretation."

"And do you?" Jane asked, nearly certain at how Lizzie would respond. "Live life to the fullest?"

Lizzie's smile faded some and she gave serious thought to her answer. "No, I wish I could be more adventurous, but I've never been a risk-taker."

Surprising. Jane didn't quite know what to say, but Lizzie bounced right back, grinning. "Besides, who would watch out for Mac? He needs me. He doesn't have anyone special in his life. And he hasn't for quite awhile. Divorced, years ago."

Jane didn't know Mac Riggs very well, but she'd

gotten the distinct impression that the big strong sheriff didn't need anyone watching out for him. He appeared quite capable in all regards, a man who didn't want or need complications in his life. He seemed to like his life just the way it was. Jane guessed that Mac kept his sister close so that he could watch out for *her,* regardless of what Lizzie might think. And she also guessed that Lizzie had sacrificed something in her life for her brother's sake.

Though it wasn't any of her business, Jane felt obligated to comment. "He's lucky to have you, Lizzie. In fact, you're lucky to have each other. I only wish I knew if I had any siblings."

Lizzie reached out to take her hand, her brown eyes warm and reassuring. "You'll get your memory back soon. It might even happen tomorrow. But in the meantime, know that you've got a friend here in Winchester."

Jane didn't know anything about herself, but she believed that she would have liked having Lizzie Riggs as her friend. "Thank you."

"Here I am, going on and on, and I haven't even asked if you'd like to get cleaned up. Would you like a hot shower or a bubble bath? I bet you'd love to get out of those clothes."

Lizzie's perception and her generous attitude made Jane feel at home. For that, she would be eternally grateful. "I would. I don't know why, but I feel like I've been in these clothes for twenty-four hours." She glanced at Lizzie, her mind whirling. "Maybe I have."

Lizzie nodded. "Maybe. All the more reason to get you out of them and into something else."

Jane had nothing else to wear, and just as she was about to relay those sentiments, Lizzie spoke up. "Let me take care of that. I've got it all under control. Just relax and enjoy. I'll show you to the bathroom. Lavender bubbles await."

Jane suddenly couldn't wait to get out of her clothes and cleaned up. And she'd learned one new thing about herself.

She preferred a steamy hot bubble bath to a shower any day of the week.

Mac entered the kitchen through the back door, unfastening his gun belt and yanking off his hat. He hooked both on a wooden rack that had seen better days. Lizzie had been pestering him about updating the kitchen, but Mac liked things as they were. Change made him uneasy, and he'd grown accustomed to the chipped tiles and outdated curtains. "Hey, Liz," he called out.

"Not Lizzie," a voice corrected, and he spun around to come face-to-face with Jane. "Just me."

He took a step back, seeing her in his kitchen, her face clean, her blond hair wet and combed back, falling to her shoulders. Those lavender eyes seemed larger now and more expressive as she examined him for a moment, before she turned toward the oven.

"Lizzie's taking a Pilates class right now. She trusted me with heating up your dinner. I hope that's okay."

Mac grunted. "Fine."

"She said not to wait dinner on her. She had some errands to do after that. Looks like you're stuck with me."

Being "stuck" watching a beautiful woman make him dinner wasn't half-bad, Mac thought. He stood there staring, watching Jane busy herself around his kitchen, wearing what he recognized as Lizzie's clothes. Levi's hugged her bottom like a baby to her mama, and the Winchester Wildcats T-shirt she wore never fit his sister that way. Lizzie was nothing if not loyal to the high school football team, but hell, Mac hadn't seen anyone fill out a T-shirt so well.

Detective skills aside, any red-blooded male would notice that Jane wasn't wearing anything under that shirt. Brown-and-white material stretched across her chest, exposing twin tips jutting outward, and each time she moved, everything jiggled.

Hell.

He wouldn't even think about what she might not be wearing under those Levi's. "More like you're stuck with me. Need some help?" he asked.

Jane stopped with oven mitts in hand, ready to put the roast in the oven. "I've got it covered. But thanks. Dinner should be ready in an hour."

He headed for the refrigerator, stifling the heat crawling up his neck, remembering why he'd come home early in the first place. He had news for Jane. "Want a beer?" he asked, yanking out a Bud.

Jane closed the oven door and stood to face him. "I don't know. Do I like beer?"

Mac grabbed a second bottle. "Only one way to find out."

He handed her a beer and gestured for her to sit at the table. Both took seats facing each other. "How're you doing? Feeling okay?" Even though she looked great, he had to ask. He felt an obligation to see to her care. And Mac never took his responsibilities lightly.

"I took a little rest earlier, and it really did me a world of good. I'm feeling much better."

"No headaches?"

Her damp hair framed her face when she shook her head. "Nope. No headaches."

Relieved, he nodded, realizing that Miss Jane Doe had been on his mind most of the day. He'd been concerned about the fall she'd taken this morning, and how she would fare the rest of the day. "I took a few deputies and went out to the site where I found you."

Jane played with her bottle, twisting it back and forth in her hands. Her eyes were wide, and Mac noted the anticipation on her face. "And?"

"Well, we can't be sure, but there's evidence that a car had pulled off the road about a mile and half back from where I found you. We found fresh tire tracks in the dirt. If it was your car, chances are it's been stolen. Then again, it could be completely unrelated."

"That's it?"

Mac shook his head. "I'm sorry it isn't better news."

Jane took a swig of her beer and Mac waited for her reaction. She kept on drinking until she'd emptied half the bottle.

"Guess you're a beer drinker, after all."

She shrugged, her eyes downcast. "So I like beer and hot bubble baths."

Mac didn't need a reminder of how Jane looked, cleaned up. He'd already had enough to deal with, watching her busy herself around the kitchen, but the thought of her naked and soaking in a steamy tub of bubbles sent his mind spinning. He took a swig of his own beer, and then a longer drink. Hell, he couldn't recall a time when a woman made him feel so unsettled. He'd taken a few jabs of ribbing at the station when he'd quit to come home early today. That teasing was bound to escalate once his deputies got a good look at her.

She peered up at him with those large questioning eyes. "What now?"

Mac returned his mind to her situation. He scratched his head, laying out his next plan of action. "Routine stuff. We'll check the local area reports of missing persons. We'll run your fingerprints tomorrow and see if we get a hit."

"Fingerprints? Do you think I could be a *felon?*" She whispered the last word, as if appalled by the notion. She had trouble meeting his gaze as she tried to mask her distress.

Mac shook his head. Instincts told him Jane Doe wasn't a criminal. He wanted to reach out to her, to reassure her and lend her comfort. But the lawman in him couldn't do it. He knew he stood behind a firm, defined line. He couldn't breach that line. Sometimes, even the most innocent-appearing people held the worst kinds of secrets. Mac had been a lawman fifteen of his thirty-five years, and he'd seen enough to harden him. "Not necessarily. Criminals aren't the only ones who get fingerprinted. We go through Automated Fingerprint Identification System, an automated way to identify persons in the military and law enforcement, too. If you've ever applied for a liquor license or been caught with a concealed weapon, your fingerprints should be on record. The system is designed for identification purposes."

"But mostly it's used to identify criminals, right?"

"Yes, that's true. Do you have a prob—"

Jane shook her head quickly. "No, no. I'm willing to do whatever it takes. I don't have a problem with that."

"Okay, that's our next step. Might take a while, so don't set yourself up for disappointment, okay?"

She nodded, and cast him a brief smile. "Okay."

Mac stood and walked toward the hall, ready to change into his street clothes. He grabbed his gun belt on the way out. Habit had him keeping the gun in his room at night, rather than out in the open where a perpetrator might find it. "Oh, one more thing," he said, turning again. Jane stood to face him, lifting her blond brows.

"Do you, um, have any unusual or identifying marks on your body?" He swept his gaze over her, unable to limit his focus to her face. Suddenly the three feet that separated them no longer seemed enough. It was one thing interviewing a victim at the jail and another thing entirely speaking of such a subject in the privacy of his own home. Or maybe it was just asking those personal questions of Jane that swamped his body with heat. "Tattoos, body piercings, anything like that?"

She shook her head. "Nothing like that. But I, uh…I do have a birthmark." She blushed, her face coloring quickly.

Encouraged, Mac asked, "Where?"

She bit her lip and turned sideways, pointing to an area just above her derriere. Lizzie's low-rise Levi's covered the spot in question. "I don't quite know how to describe it. It's kinda hard for me to see."

Mac swallowed, cursing himself for asking the question in the first place. Always the dutiful lawman… He stood there, staring at Jane's perfect butt.

"Is it important?" she asked, "because you could— I mean, I would let…"

Mac stared into clear blue, earnest eyes. He stepped back, shaking his head. "I've tangled with some pretty tough characters, Jane, but sorry. I'm just not that brave." Or stupid, he wanted to add.

He exited the room quickly, his body tight and hot, but even worse, his ears burning with Jane's quiet chuckling.

Three

"I gathered my things, if you want to take a look at them," Jane said, holding the pile of newly laundered clothes. She stood by the screen door, waiting for Mac's response.

He sat comfortably in a white wooden lawn chair, looking out at the backyard garden, which was full of trimmed shrubs and colorful spring flowers that Lizzie prided herself on. She'd given Jane a quick tour of the grounds when they'd met earlier today.

Lizzie had been kind enough to wash and dry all of her clothes, except, of course, the cashmere sweater. It was ruined anyway, ripped a bit and stained with red dirt from when she'd fallen.

After dinner, Mac had asked to see Jane's belongings, meager as they were.

"Bring them outside," he said now. "It's a nice night. I made coffee."

The screen door slammed shut behind her as she exited the house. Two mugs of coffee sat on a white wicker table beside Mac. She took the other seat, somewhat touched that he had included her in his little respite.

"I can vouch for my coffee. I make a mean cup."

"That's good, I think," she murmured, setting her clothes on her lap.

Mac cleaned up nicely, she thought. She'd been taken aback earlier this evening when he'd entered the kitchen for dinner dressed in casual street clothes—faded jeans and a black polo shirt. Tanned and well muscled, he seemed less formidable out of his uniform, but just as appealing.

She wondered what it would take to bring down his guard. She had yet to see him smile.

"I have to thank you again for all you're doing for me."

"It's my—"

"And don't say it's your job, Sheriff Riggs," she interrupted, wagging a finger at him. "You went beyond the call of duty by taking me in. You have a lovely home and your sister is as friendly as can be. Both of you have made me so welcome. Under the circumstances, I feel pretty lucky. One day I hope to find a way to make it up to you."

Mac glanced at her, his dark brows arching. His lips quirked and he shook his head. "Don't offer to show me your birthmark again and we'll call it even."

Completely stunned, Jane gasped, barely managing to utter the words, "My birthmark? I thought it would... help," she said, her voice rising once again as she nearly bounded from her chair. The only thing stopping her were the clothes on her lap, which she tried darn hard not to drop. "I would never have made that offer if I wasn't desperate to find out who I am, you idiot." She barely contained her temper, but she did take a swat at his arm. His well-honed instincts must have kicked in, because he jerked away quickly.

Mac laughed then, a full-out, deep laugh, and the change in his face was astounding—so much so that for a moment Jane forgot all about her anger. She stared at him, her heart doing major flips. Oh God, she thought wryly, he's gorgeous. Amazing.

"Don't get me wrong, Jane. It's the best offer I've had in five years."

Jane sank back down in her seat, staring at him and shaking her head. "Only five?" she said with sarcasm. Despite her cutting remark, she was still awed by the transformation on the lawman's face. And the fact that he had stayed single all this time.

Mac took hold of the clothes she'd brought outside, removing them from her lap. "Beer, bubble baths and bad temper. At least we're learning something about you, Jane."

She countered quickly, "And to think I was beginning to believe the good sheriff wasn't human."

Where had that come from? Jane chided herself on her cynical tongue. The words just poured out of her. And she learned that when backed in a corner, she came out fighting.

Mac's smile faded and he pierced her with dark probing

eyes. He spoke in a low, sexy tone, more like a whisper meant for her ears alone. "Believe me, I'm human. That birthmark of yours will be in my dreams tonight."

He kept his eyes focused on hers, but the heat of his stare and the implication of his words poured through her like molten lava.

"Oh," she said quietly, fully aware of the sparks igniting between them. But it seemed they both came to their senses at the same time. They leaned back in their chairs, and Mac began examining her clothes.

The moment had come and gone, and Jane was grateful. She didn't need any complications right now. Admitting that Mac Riggs was an interesting and appealing man was one thing, but allowing anything to develop between them was something else again. How could she? She didn't know who she was or where she belonged.

"Lizzie said your clothes were high-end." Mac became all business again, studying the designer label on her jeans.

"I suppose."

He ran his hands up and down the material, then looked inside the waistband.

"Size five."

Jane rolled her eyes. Didn't the man know not to announce to the world a woman's dress size? After her last few sardonic remarks to him, she decided not to comment.

"Why do women spend a fortune on Gucci and Guess and Ralph Lauren, when Levi's works just fine?" He glanced at her jeans and nodded.

"Maybe because women want to look better than 'just fine.'"

Mac grunted.

Then he lifted her watch and brought it close to his face, examining the diamond. "Pretty good size diamond in there." He flipped it over. "No inscription."

He set the pants and the watch on the table and moved on to examine her sweater. "Why would you be wearing a sweater, cashmere no less, in the middle of June?"

She shrugged, her frustration mounting. Nothing in her possession seemed to lead to any clues as to her identity. "I don't know, but I got the feeling that I'd been in my clothes a long time."

"Meaning?"

"That maybe I slept in them. Or traveled in them a long while. I'm not sure."

Mac drew oxygen into his lungs. "Maybe. That could mean you came a long way. If you traveled during the night, you'd most likely need warmer clothes. That would explain the sweater. And the fact that you don't know much about Colorado in June. Hell, it gets sweltering hot here during the day this time of year."

"That's not much to go on, is it?"

Mac sipped his coffee, staring out into his backyard, contemplating. "It's something, at least."

Then he glanced her way. "For what it's worth, I don't think you're from this area at all."

"Why?"

"Just a hunch." Then he lifted her wide, black suede belt and studied it. "This isn't a western belt. Won't fit through any loops. In fact, it looks pretty darn expensive."

Jane didn't have any answers. She couldn't respond.

She felt at such a loss, as if trying to put together a puzzle where none of the pieces seemed to fit.

She took her first sip of Mac's mean cup of coffee. "Not bad, Sheriff Riggs."

"Is there a compliment somewhere in there?"

"I won't lie. This is good coffee."

He nodded, sipping from his own cup. "Thanks."

He set the belt down beside the rest of her things and stood up. Jane hadn't the nerve to let him see her underwear. She'd kept them hidden in her room. She couldn't stand to let Mac know that she'd worn a teeny, minuscule scrap of material that one might mistake as underpants.

That was just too much information for the sheriff to have.

"I'll take you by the station in the morning and we'll get started on your case."

Jane rose, picking up her things and hugging them to her chest. They were all she had in the world right now. She felt the evening coming to an end, and she needed the comfort. "Okay."

"Well, good night." Mac tipped his head in a brief nod of farewell.

But Jane couldn't let him go. Not before she apologized. She'd been out of line, and he deserved more for all he'd done for her. "Wait. I, uh, can't say good night without apologizing for how I behaved earlier."

Mac smiled then, with a quick flash of white teeth and full lips. "Don't apologize, Jane. I haven't had a good laugh in way too long."

"Really?" she asked, puzzled. "What was so funny?"

"You," he said. "No one's dared call me an *idiot* since I was nine years old. Back then, I bloodied the kid's nose and got sent to the principal's office."

"Oh," she said, realizing her sharp tongue had indeed insulted the sheriff. "Now I really feel bad."

Mac grabbed her hand and squeezed, ready to say something. But just then they heard a car pull up. "That'll be Lizzie," he said, dropping her hand and stepping back. And within a minute, Lizzie had their full attention.

"I guessed at the size," Mac's sister said, displaying half a dozen items of lingerie that she'd purchased for Jane. She'd also bought a hairbrush, comb and tooth-brush, as well as a small travel kit filled with lotion and shampoo, lip gloss and other makeup essentials. "You needed some things of your own, especially something to wear to bed tonight."

Jane cleared her throat, glancing at the personal items Lizzie had laid out on the kitchen table as Mac lodged himself against the counter, watching. So many emotions whirled around inside her that she had trouble naming them all—gratitude, for one, but embarrassment as well, along with an uncanny sense of helplessness. "I don't know what to say. I can't possibly pay for these right now."

"It's okay, Jane. Call it a loan. Besides," Lizzie said, looking over Jane's head to wink at her brother, "I put them all on Mac's credit card."

Jane whipped her head around to find him shrugging.

Lizzie took her hand and squeezed gently. "It's okay. Mac's got more money than Donald Trump. The only difference is that my brother doesn't flaunt what he has. He can afford it."

Jane eyed the pretty pink nightie, a matching light-weight robe and four pair of underpants, each a different style, from full cotton panties to a lacy red thong, with the others in between.

"I didn't know your preference," Lizzie explained.

"Oh, Lizzie. This is so thoughtful and generous. They're all perfect. Thank you," she said, then turned again to catch Mac's stare. "And I'll find a way to pay you back."

He shook his head. "Don't worry about that right now."

"As soon as I can, I'm taking you shopping," Lizzie said. "You'll need more than my hand-me-downs to wear."

"I don't mind," Jane said, feeling overwhelmed. She didn't have any means to pay either of them back for their kindness and generosity. Lizzie's clothes fit her well enough, even though they were a tad on the tight side. "Besides, I'm hoping to get my memory back before there's a need to go on a shopping spree."

Lizzie smiled warmly. "I hope so, too, Jane. But just in case, we'll make a day of it, sometime soon. Right now, I'm knee-deep in finals. School will out by the end of the week, and after that I'll have some free time."

Jane hoped with her whole heart it wouldn't come to that. She hoped to regain her memory very soon. But Lizzie seemed intent on planning a shopping day, and the last thing Jane wanted to do was discourage her enthusiasm. "Okay, then, I'll look forward to it."

Mac's sister beamed. "Good."

"Thank you, Lizzie. I think I'll take my things and head off to bed. I have to be up at the crack of dawn. Mac is taking me to the station tomorrow to get finger-printed." She turned to him. "Shall I set my alarm?"

He came forward, his gaze focused on the red thong panty atop her stack of new lingerie. "I'll give a knock at your door when it's time. No need to get up too early." His gaze finally rose to meet hers, and the unmistakable gleam in his dark eyes was enough to send Jane off to bed with a bad case of tingles.

"Rise and shine, Miss Doe," Mac said from outside Jane's door. His knocking had woken her from a sound sleep. She opened her eyes slowly and lay there, allow-ing the events of the last twenty-four hours to sink in. She knew she'd slept in a strange bed, but oddly enough, she'd fallen asleep almost immediately. And she'd dreamed.

She'd hoped to dream about something from her past, something that would give her a clue as to her identity, but that hadn't been the case at all.

She stared up at the ceiling, hugging her pillow. "I dreamed of Sheriff Mac Riggs," she whispered incred-ulously. And she recalled her dream vividly, almost a complete replay of how Mac had found her lying in the dirt up on that canyon road. She'd dreamed of him holding her in his arms, bringing her to safety, but that was where the dream got fuzzy.

She'd woken up awash with warmth.

"Jane, did you hear me?"

"Oh, yes," she said, recognizing that familiar deep voice from her dream last night. "I'm awake. I'll be dressed in a few minutes."

"Take your time. Coffee's brewing in the kitchen," he called through her door. "Help yourself to breakfast. Lizzie had to rush off to school early. I'll be in the garage."

"Okay," she said, then added quietly, "Thanks."

Lizzie had left a few tank tops and several blouses on her dresser. Jane decided the black blouse with lacy trim would look a little more appropriate for the sheriff's station than the hot-pink or lime-green tank tops. She slipped out of her nightgown and into the borrowed clothes. Jane opted for her own boots this time, feeling more comfortable in them than the tennis shoes Lizzie had provided.

Jane took a look at herself in the mirror, hoping that something more than lavender-blue eyes and blond hair would register, but nothing came to mind. She recognized the face staring back at her, but that was all. No past, no history. It was as if her life had begun the minute Mac had found her up on that road. She promised herself to keep positive and remain patient. She trusted Mac Riggs, and placed her faith in him. And she prayed that something would turn up today.

She took a minute to brush her hair, apply lip gloss and brush a few swipes of mascara on her eyelashes. She made up the bed and tidied the room, then headed to the kitchen. She could really use a big cup of Mac's mean coffee.

Jane stopped short when she entered the kitchen. The table was set for one, complete with napkin and place mat, even a thin-stemmed red rose in a tall glass vase. Eggs, bacon, oatmeal and biscuits were laid out in bowls, buffet style. Jane shook her head. She couldn't possibly eat all this food.

The rich scent of coffee filled the room and she poured herself a cup, then sat down, once again overwhelmed. She filled half a bowl with oatmeal and ate it quickly, then covered the rest of the food with foil and placed it in the refrigerator.

She took a second to savor the sweet scent of the rose, a thoughtful gesture on Mac's part, then poured a second mug of coffee, and with two mugs in hand, strode purposefully out the back door to the garage.

Coffee spilled from the mugs when she stopped suddenly, realizing her mistake. "Oh, uh, sorry. I didn't mean to interrupt."

She glanced at the coffee stains on the garage floor, cursing her own stupidity for seeking Mac out.

"Hey, Jane," he said. "Morning. And you're not interrupting. I'm almost through."

Jane shot him a half smile, trying not to stare, but it wasn't easy, seeing him in a pair of gray sweatpants and nothing else, lifting weights. Beads of perspiration coated his bare chest and his skin gleamed in the morning light filtering into the garage. His arms bunched and muscles popped as he finished his repetitions with arm weights.

Pulse racing, Jane set the mugs down on a worktable,

fearing she'd drop them otherwise. Pumped up and hard, Mac was the most physically fit man she'd ever seen.

So *that* was what lay beneath his tan-and-brown sheriff's uniform.

Jane's mouth went dry. She sipped her coffee, acting nonchalant and trying to keep her focus. She'd come out here for a reason. Ogling the sheriff hadn't been her intent, yet she couldn't deny the attraction. She felt drawn to Mac Riggs and that wasn't a good thing.

Mac finished his workout and sat down on a bench, wiping sweat from his brow. Jane watched him swipe at his torso with a small white towel. "I want to thank you for breakfast," she stated quickly. "I ate oatmeal. I guess I'm not much of a breakfast eater."

He swept a long, leisurely look over her body. Heat crawled up her neck and suddenly she felt self-conscious in Lizzie's tight clothes.

"Guess not. I should have known."

"Now we do know."

"Right," he said, his gaze lifting from her chest to her eyes.

"I guess you don't need coffee," she said lamely, showing him the mug.

He brought a big bottle of water to his lips and took a swig. "No, but thanks for the thought."

"Speaking of thoughtful," she said, "I really liked the red rose. Is it from your garden?"

He sipped water again, and Jane watched his throat work, taking it in. "Lizzie's doing. I cook. She sets the table. She loves her flowers."

"Oh," Jane said, kicking herself for the assumption. Of course Mac wasn't the sentimental or romantic type. Why would he have put that rose on the table for her? She was his houseguest, not his lover. "I'll have to thank her. So is this your hobby?"

Mac glanced around the garage at his workout stations. Jane figured he had half a regular gym in here, from free weights to Nautilus machines, mats and benches.

"It's my job," he said, and when he met Jane's eyes, she chuckled.

He cracked a smile and she realized that they had their own private joke. "Okay, I have to keep fit for work. It's just easier doing it at home, on my own schedule. And I guess I do enjoy it. I run through a thirty minute workout most mornings before work, and when I'm off duty, I go an hour or two."

Jane swept another gaze around the garage. "For a home gym, it's quite impressive." And so was he.

Mac nodded. "Thanks. You know, not that you need it, but you're welcome to use my equipment anytime you want. It's always good to stay in shape."

"You are," she blurted, and then caught herself. She added quickly, "Very nice to offer. Maybe I will sometime."

Use your equipment. Oh boy, Jane, she thought. Get out of here before you make a complete fool of yourself.

"What time will you be ready?" she asked.

"Give me ten minutes to take a quick shower, then we'll be out of here."

"Okay, fine. I'll meet you inside."

And she made herself a mental note not to go traipsing after Mac Riggs when he worked out in the garage. It was far too dangerous.

Four

Half a dozen deputies huddled around Jane, waiting on introductions. "Back off," Mac said. "Give the lady some breathing room."

The deputies didn't budge, except to bump each other as they offered handshakes and made small talk with her. Deputy Sheriff Marion Sheaver, his favorite colleague, if the crustiest deputy on the force, pulled him aside. She was six months from retirement and always had an opinion.

"She's beautiful," she said, "and quite a big deal around here. It's been a slow week and a mysterious woman with no memory can liven things up. Let the boys talk to her. I bet she could use some new friends."

"Friends?" Mac glared at his deputies, trying to shake

off the protective feelings he had for Jane. She was his responsibility, nothing more. But sensations whirled through him as he watched his men gawk at her as if she were some prize to be won at the county fair. "I doubt *friendship* is on their minds."

"And what about you, Mac? What's on your mind?"

"She's just a case, Marion."

"You took her in," she said, raising her graying brows. "She's living with you."

"Me and Lizzie. And don't forget, when I found her she had no memory, no money, no identification. She's not the type of woman to go into a shelter, for Pete's sake. She was pretty freaked out about her situation."

Marion scratched her head and eyed him. Mac always hated that particular look on her face. It usually meant a lecture was coming. Or an opinion he didn't want to hear. "She's beautiful."

Mac folded his arms, ready for battle. "You said that already."

"You like her."

"I don't know her. Hell, *she* doesn't know her. Jane's got amnesia, remember. She's just learning about herself."

"Mac, it's about time you got involved with a woman again. If not your Jane Doe, then someone else." Marion shook her finger at him. "You're too good a man to live alone."

He rolled his eyes. "Not this again."

"You had a bad experience, but that was years ago."

"Deputy Sheaver, don't go there."

"Don't pull rank on me, Mac. You know I'm gunning for you."

"Yeah, it's your mission in life to see me tied down before you retire."

"And let Lizzie have a life of her own."

Mac's eyes went wide. "I'm not stopping her from anything. She's a grown woman. She can do anything she wants."

Marion shook her head and closed her eyes briefly. "If you believe that, then you're missing all the clues. And for a man in your profession, that's a real crime."

Mac stalked off, heading for Jane, parting his men and taking her arm. "Ready?" he asked her, making eye contact with each one of his deputies. Funny thing, but the only men seeking out her "friendship" were his unattached bachelor deputies. "Let's get those fingerprints now."

He glanced at his staff. "Don't you have work to do?"

Jane smiled at the officers. "Nice meeting you all."

Mac grunted as the men slowly made their back to their desks.

"Is everyone in Winchester County so nice?" Jane asked, and Mac realized that she had no clue as to how attractive she was. He found that quality endearing. He wondered if she came by that trait naturally, or was it due to her recent memory loss? Who was the real Jane Doe? And why was it so hard containing his attraction to her?

"Nosy is what I'd call them. Good men, each one, but your appearance here in Winchester has caused quite a stir."

"Really? Why?"

Mac shrugged, then placing his hand on the small of her back, led her down the hallway to be fingerprinted. Maybe they'd get lucky and get a hit before the end of the day. Then this unsettled feeling he'd been experiencing would disappear—when Jane left town.

"It's a small community. We get petty thefts and local disputes, but we've never had an amnesia victim show up on our doorstep. You're quite a mystery."

"I wish I wasn't."

"Maybe we'll have some luck through AFIS. Let's hope for good news."

"But what if that doesn't work? What if my fingerprints aren't in there?"

Mac halted, hearing the slight desperation in her voice. "Don't worry, Jane. There's more to do. We have a protocol. The next step would be to go to the local media. That's why I asked about identifying marks on your, uh, body." Mac immediately recalled their conversation about Jane's birthmark. He hadn't dreamed of it or her, like he'd said last night, but the woman had never been far from his mind since he'd met her, birthmark and all.

Jane's blond brows rose to attention and she had this uncanny way of raising one brow higher than the other that drove him wild. "You mean for me to go on television?"

"Not exactly. We'd release a picture of you for the newspapers and television stations, along with what we know about you. We'd do spots on local radio stations as well, with your description and details about how you were found. We'd publicize anything that would help someone identify you."

"Oh, when would we do that?"

"We can do so as soon as I can make the arrangements."

"What do you think I should do?" she asked, looking up at him with those big blue eyes. It was clear that she trusted him, and he didn't want to abuse that trust.

Mac placed his hand on her back again and they began walking slowly. "I say go for it. The more we do, the faster we can get results. I only hesitated about the media because being exposed like that tends to make some people uncomfortable. We can wait on it and hope you remember something, or we can move straight ahead."

Jane listened intently, then nodded. "Let's move ahead. And I hate to be a pessimist, but what if nothing works?"

Mac held her stare, reassuring her. "There's more to do if we come up empty with all of this."

"Like what?"

"DNA samples, hypnotist… But let's not jump the gun. I'll explain all this to you later." He stopped again once they reached the window whose sign read Fingerprints. "Here we are. Margie will take you through the process. I'll be in my office. Check with me when you're through."

Jane nodded and Mac left her, heading back to his office. Jane was one concern, but now Marion had planted a bug in his head about Lizzie.

And it was all Mac could think about the rest of the day.

"You're home earlier than I expected," Lizzie said, as she set down a mass of papers on the entry table and walked over to the living room sofa. Jane had spent the bulk of the afternoon reading. She'd found a Dean

Koontz novel on the fireplace mantel and figured it would be a good way to pass the time.

"Hi, Lizzie. I could say the same about you. Finals all through for the day?" She set the book down, happy to have Lizzie's company for the moment.

"Yep, and I thought I'd bring the essays home, rather than read them in the classroom. This way I can get comfy and put my feet up. Makes for a more generous grade for my students." She grinned.

"I bet you're pretty generous to them, anyway. What subjects do you teach?"

Lizzie sat down next to her on the sofa and sighed. "What subjects don't I teach? I've been around a while and I've taught everything from home economics and art to journalism and English. Right now I'm teaching tenth grade English and history."

"Wow, that's pretty impressive. Do you have a favorite subject?"

"Mmm, I love American history. But it's a challenge getting my students excited about our heritage."

Jane couldn't remember her school days, so she had little to add. She didn't know her favorite subject or whether she had appreciated American history while she was in school.

"How was your day?" Lizzie asked, making herself comfortable on the sofa. She kicked off her sandals and lifted her legs, tucking her feet under her. Her earnest approach and guileless nature was what Jane liked best about Lizzie Riggs. She felt immediate warmth and a budding friendship with her.

"My day went well. Your brother's doing all he can for me. I spent the morning getting fingerprinted, and then Mac had me go through some missing persons reports. I guess time will tell. But I did meet some of the nicest deputies today. Everyone seemed so friendly. One of the men asked about you. A Lyle Brody?"

Lizzie's brown eyes rounded in surprise and her voice went raspy. "*Lyle* asked for me?"

It seemed that Lizzie's whole demeanor changed then. Her face lit up like a Christmas tree and she sat up, leaning in, on full alert. Her body language couldn't be mistaken. Lizzie had the hots for Lyle Brody.

"He sure did. He said to say hello and that you should stop by the jail again real soon."

Lizzie's face took on a dreamy quality. "He didn't."

Jane grinned. "He did. He also said that I was lucky to be staying with you, because you're the best cook in Winchester County. Did you cook for him?"

Lizzie beamed, though she tried darn hard to hide the fact. "Well, yes. But not really. I mean to say, Mac started this thing at the jail. The last Friday of every month they have Potluck Pantry. He's got so many darn bachelors on the force that he decided once a month his deputies should get a decent meal. So some of us pitch in and cook them up enough food for lunch and dinner."

"That's nice. And Lyle likes your cooking in particular?"

Lizzie shrugged modestly. "I suppose."

Jane figured Lizzie to be in her late twenties. She was cute and friendly and had a great personality. There had to be a reason why she wasn't married, or at least dating. And Jane had a feeling that the reason had to do with Mac. Lizzie had made a comment once before about her loyalty to her brother.

"So, if he likes your cooking so much, why not cook him up a meal…in private?" Jane pressed.

Lizzie nodded. "I've thought about it, hundreds of times, but…"

"But?"

"It's complicated."

"So, un-complicate it."

"If only Mac would settle down again," she said quietly, and Jane guessed that she hadn't meant her comment to be heard.

"Mac is a big boy, Lizzie," Jane said sweetly. She didn't want to overstep her bounds, but she also wanted to help her new friend.

"I know. But he's taken care of me for fifteen years. I can't abandon him now. I can't…leave my brother alone."

"Have you spoken to him about this?"

Lizzie shook her head. "No. Mac's protective. You know, the big brother syndrome. He doesn't think anyone's good enough for me. He's kind of in the stone age about things like that."

"Maybe it's time you shook him into the twenty-first century."

Lizzie took a good long minute to think about it, then smiled, her face beaming again. She gave Jane the oddest look and patted her knee. "Maybe I should. Thanks, Jane. I think you've hit upon something here."

She grabbed her essay papers and sighed with contentment. "I'll be hibernating in my room for two hours, then I'm off. I have a dinner meeting tonight. I'll be home kind of late. You don't mind cooking a meal for Mac, do you?"

"No," Jane said, watching her leave the room with a bounce in her step. "Of course not."

The strangest sensation swept over Jane. She shuddered involuntarily. Relying on her powers of deduction as well as a gut feeling, she surmised that something significant had just happened, something to do with her and Lizzie's hunky brother.

Mac entered the kitchen and cursed under his breath. "Where the hell is Lizzie?"

"What?" Jane turned around from her task at the kitchen counter, looking puzzled. "Did you say something?"

"It's nothing," he answered, hanging up his hat and gun belt on the hook by the door. He already knew the answer. Lizzie's car wasn't in the driveway and she wouldn't be home for dinner tonight. Again. This made three consecutive nights that she had been long gone when he arrived home from work.

Mac knew exactly what his little sister was up to. Lizzie and Marion had been prodding him for years to get involved with a woman again. Lizzie's absence again tonight, the fact that she'd chosen the most revealing clothes to give Jane to wear, the fact that Jane looked like a damn cover model in those clothes, all had Mac's nerves on edge.

Yeah, he knew what Lizzie was up to—and it was working.

Damn. Spending a good part of his days with Jane and the better part of the evenings hadn't helped his resolve to keep his distance. He was drawn to her like a moth to a flame.

Tomorrow her picture would be splashed all over the television screens and newspapers. Her description would air on the local radio stations as well. Soon Jane Doe would be a household name in Winchester County.

But right now she stood in his kitchen, looking too much like she belonged there, cooking up his dinner.

Mac took a big breath to steady his nerves. Jane caught his deep sigh, and so he said quickly, "Something smells good."

She smiled and even the specks of flour dusting her face couldn't mar her beauty. Her clothes fit her like a glove. Lizzie's Levi's hugged her hips, and Jane wore a white, sleeveless button-down blouse two sizes too small for her, each button seeming to strain to keep the material from separating. Mac had had trouble keeping his eyes averted today at the jail, and he couldn't miss his deputies' conspicuous interest, either. Jane turned heads wherever she went. He had to do something about her attire. She was pretty enough to draw attention without those revealing clothes, but with them, Mac hated to admit, the woman turned him on.

He forced his body not to react while at work. But seeing her in his kitchen, and being alone with her, well, hell. He was human. And hard as a rock.

"It's nothing special, just baked chicken and potatoes. I tried making biscuits, too. I'm sure you'd prefer Lizzie's cooking over mine."

Mac ran his hand through his short-cropped hair. "Same restaurant, different chef. Good cooking is good cooking, Jane. I'll be back in a few minutes to help set the table."

With that, Mac headed for an ice-cold shower.

Thirty minutes later, he entered the kitchen again after the icy assault and the stern, wordless lecture he'd given himself. He felt relieved and much more in control.

He could manage living with the lovely blonde without getting personally involved. He knew something of self-discipline.

Until he took one look at Jane's face.

She turned to him from the stove, her face flushed, her eyes moist and her body trembling.

The smoke alarm began to chirp wildly.

He glanced down at the pan of chicken, the charred and blackened pieces almost unrecognizable now, surrounded by twice crisped potatoes and toasted biscuits that would chew like leather. The house smelled like a Wildcats football rally bonfire—after the fact—and was just as smoky.

Mac grimaced at the scene, feeling things he had no right feeling. Caring too much. He'd never been one to lose his heart to a woman. Not even his one-time wife.

"Jane, what the hell?"

Upon hearing her name, she burst into tears. Her body shuddered uncontrollably and she broke down, crying quietly. Her silent sobs wrenched his heart.

He reached for the kitchen window, sliding it open quickly, and smoke found its way out. He turned to her. "It's just dinner," he said roughly. "We'll get pizza."

"I…told you, Lizzie's a better cook. I…don't…know what I'm doing here," she managed to blubber, waving her arms in the air.

"Okay, so maybe Lizzie's a better cook. Maybe cooking isn't your thing."

"It's not just dinner…you, you…"

"Idiot?"

"I didn't call you an idiot. I learned my lesson the first time."

"But you were thinking it."

Jane sopped up her tears then glared with those lavender-blue eyes that went dollar size on him.

"What?" he growled. What the hell had he done wrong?

She tossed the kitchen towel at him.

Surprised at her gumption, he caught the towel before it slammed into his face. "Damn it, Jane. I can't figure you out."

"That makes two of us!" Her breaths shaky, she continued, "I can't figure me out, either! I don't know a thing about myself. I can't cook worth a darn, that's a given. But what else do I know? Nothing. Not one darn thing."

Mac played with the kitchen towel, which sported blue ducks and yellow daisies. Jane had a temper. She had spirit and pride and intelligence. He already knew she was a knockout in the looks department. His mind in turmoil, he couldn't tell if he was more pissed off or more aroused.

Neither emotion would do.

"Is all this about one burned dinner?" he asked, trying to make some sense of her outburst. He couldn't claim to know what she was going through right now, but he'd done and would do everything in his power to help her regain her memory.

She pursed her lips and shook her head.

"No? Then what?"

Jane lowered her head, her eyes downcast, as if staring at the ruined meal, but Mac knew she didn't really see any of it. "Deputy Brody called while you were in the shower. He said…he said that, uh, my fingerprints didn't come up with a match. I was supposed to relay the message."

Damn, Lyle should have run that by me privately.

When she glanced at him this time with a face devoid of hope, a body slumped in defeat, Mac couldn't hold back another second. He took the steps necessary to reach her. He swept her into his arms, pulling her close, resting her head against his chest and tucking her hair under his chin.

"It's okay, Jane," he whispered, brushing his lips to her forehead. "Don't give up hope."

She clung to him, and he realized that maybe this had been what she needed all along—someone to hold her. To tell her everything was going to be all right.

He glanced down to where her breasts crushed against him. The top button of her blouse popped open, exposing creamy skin, right down to the white lace bra she wore.

He slid his eyes shut, but her image, and the sweet

fragrant scent of her hair, sent him over the edge. He was rock solid against her and didn't give a damn.

"Mac," she whispered softly.

When he looked down he met her gaze, and Mac realized it wasn't just comfort Jane wanted. He tipped her head and bent his, watching acceptance and desire sweep across Jane's lovely face. He brought his lips down on hers, claiming her mouth in a kiss that began slowly, softly, a test to where they would go from there. A little throaty sound slipped from Jane's lips and Mac drew her closer, cupping her face in his hands, then sliding them farther back, to flow through her blond waves.

She pressed in, wrapping her arms around his neck, her fingers digging into his hair. Her mouth was soft and warm and giving, and Mac deepened the kiss, exploring her lips thoroughly until she sighed with pleasure.

He hadn't been with a woman in quite a while. Fact was, he'd dated some, slept with others, but he couldn't recall a time when a woman had crept into his bones like this. He couldn't remember ever needing this way.

He parted Jane's lips and kissed her openmouthed, losing some of his usual self-control as their tongues danced together, a gentle ballet that soon became a wild tango. Lips and tongues and bodies touched and meshed and blended. They created heat together, a blaze that brought sweat to their brows. Hearts pounded. Bodies cried out for more.

A thought struck Mac. He pulled back, breaking off the kiss, and looked deeply into Jane's eyes. "You could be married."

She shook her head, lifting her left hand and wiggling her ringless ring finger. "I don't think so."

"You could be engaged. Maybe there's a man out there waiting to marry you."

Again, Jane shook her head. "There's no one. Don't ask me how I know, I just do."

Mac wasn't so sure. Jane Doe didn't appear to be a woman who'd be alone in the world. She'd shown him passion and vulnerability, as well as strength and intelligence. She was beautiful and sexy and feisty as hell. How could a woman like that be unattached?

She still had her arms around his neck. Mac relished their contact one minute more, taking her in another deep, long, deliberate kiss, before he reached down to the slope of her breasts.

She waited, her expectant gaze fastened to his. Mac touched the top button that had popped open. She took in a deep breath, straining the material even more. He hesitated, realizing the implications of his next move. He wanted nothing more than to slip his hands inside her blouse and stroke her flesh. To feel the soft, ripe swells.

Slowly, with deft fingers, he refastened the button and backed away. He blinked from the impact of leaving her, giving up the best gift he might ever receive. Clearing his throat, he lifted his gaze to look into her baffled blue eyes. "Tomorrow, we go shopping. You need clothes of your own."

Five

"Well, here we are," Mac said as he pulled into the Winchester Mall parking lot. "It's not fancy, but I think you'll find something you might like here."

Jane glanced at him, sitting in his black Trailblazer, looking as if he wished he were anywhere but here. He wore blue jeans that fit him too well and a white tank with four large brown initials, WCSD. Winchester County Sheriff's Department.

She decided Mac Riggs was one with his job. Whether off duty or on, his job, his commitment to the county, defined him. She respected him for his dedication and knew she was nothing more to him than an obligation.

But she hadn't felt like an obligation when he'd kissed her last night. She been swamped with emotions, wondering about herself, struggling with the meal. And when Deputy Brody had called with the disappointing news, Jane had gone into meltdown.

She hadn't expected to fall into Mac's arms that way, or to kiss him for all she was worth. She hadn't expected to feel more alive in that moment than she had for the last four days, ever since she'd woken up with no memory.

The kiss had been wonderful, but it had caused them awkward moments the rest of the evening. They'd shared a pizza, perhaps to prove to each other that they could handle what had happened, or rather *not* happened, between them. But their stolen looks, averted glances and stilted conversations had sent Jane to bed early.

For both of their sakes.

Yet she couldn't deny she'd wanted to curl up next to Mac on her bed. She wanted his arms around her, comforting her and making her feel alive and vital once again.

"This is going beyond the call, Mac. I bet this is the last place you want to be on your day off."

Mac glanced at her lime-green tank top, his eyes holding begrudged appreciation. "It's necessary."

"But Lizzie said if you'd only waited until the weekend, she would be happy to take me."

Mac bounded out of his car, slamming the door. He came around to her side quickly and opened hers. "Necessary for my general health, Jane."

His brows rose and he shot her a direct look. She glanced down, seeing herself as he might see her. True, she'd felt packed into her clothes like a sardine, but she hadn't realized how that might make her appear to Mac.

Up until last night she hadn't thought he'd even given her a second look.

"You've got a body on you," Mac said, walking toward the mall entrance. "And I'd rather not be reminded of it every time I look at you."

Jane stepped down from the Trailblazer, slamming the door also, nearly having to break into a run to catch up with him. He'd infuriated her with that last comment. As if Jane had had a choice in the matter! She'd been left with only the clothes on her back. She couldn't help it that Lizzie's wardrobe didn't quite fit right. Jane would have seemed ungrateful to complain.

"That shouldn't bother you, Sheriff. You've got enough willpower for both of us."

Mac slanted her a look. "Don't be too sure of it."

"Is that all it takes to get you interested?"

He stopped in his tracks and stared at her. "What?"

Flushed now and nearly out of breath, Jane said softly, "I think you heard me."

"I *can't* be interested, Jane. Don't you get that? You're living under my roof, under my protection. Whether you think so or not, you may have ties to other people. People who love and care for you."

"Yes, I get that. I *got* that last night. You made yourself pretty clear."

Mac shook his head, his expression grim. Jane frustrated him, and she was beginning to understand why. He protected his heart well. So well that he wouldn't even open up enough to take a chance. His dedication to his profession wouldn't allow him to compromise his position. She *got* all of that.

But she also *got* that he had everything to lose. What if she had a past, a family who was looking for her? What if she had a man searching for her? Jane could only see the small details of her life now, living here in Winchester, but Mac could see the whole picture.

She couldn't blame him for backing off. She took hold of his hand and gave a gentle squeeze. "Listen, I'm sorry. I owe you so much for everything you've done."

"You don't owe me, Jane."

"I do. And today, well, you're doing such a nice thing by taking me shopping. Let's not argue. Let's get this over with. I promise I'll be fast. I won't prolong the torture."

Mac grinned then, a quick lifting of the corners of his mouth. His teeth flashed, white and straight and her heart did that thing again. Mac had a killer smile.

"You're really something, Jane Doe."

She cocked her head to one side. "Do you really have Trump money?"

He laughed. "Nobody has Trump money."

"Don't worry, I'll go easy on your wallet."

He placed his hand on her back and led her inside the Winchester Mall. "I'll bet you a week's worth of laundry duty you'll empty me out within an hour."

"Deal."

"Hey, you're that woman with no memory, right? I saw your picture on the news early this morning," the young salesgirl announced, scrutinizing Jane's face. "You were found up by Deerlick Canyon. What's it like, not remembering who you are?"

Jane's expression faltered for a moment. "Well, I, uh, it's not something I would wish on anybody."

Mac stepped up to the sales counter, presenting his credit card. "All through here?" he asked.

The salesgirl, who was named Luanne, according to the pink tag pinned to her chest, took the credit card. "I heard you were injured, but no one really knows how." She glanced at Mac's card, then nodded. "Oh, you're the one who found her. The news said to contact the sheriff's department if anyone recognizes you."

"Yes, that's right," Jane said, her body language telling Mac that she wanted out of this conversation.

"Well, I don't." Again, Luanne studied Jane's face. "Nope. I don't recognize you. Can't say that you've ever been in our store before."

"Thank you. We'll keep that in mind. Could you hurry up with that," Mac said, pointing to the card and the clothes Jane had set on the counter. "We've got a lot to do this morning."

"Oh, sure." Luanne popped her bubble gum a few times as she rang up the sale, and had Mac sign for the purchases. "I bet someone recognizes you, though. I saw your picture on the front lawn as I was pulling out of my garage."

"On your front lawn?" Jane asked.

"Front page of the *Winchester Chronicle*. Boy, I can't imagine. Must be kinda strange."

Jane sent her a weak smile. "It's very strange."

Luanne slipped the clothes into a shiny black bag and handed Mac his credit card and Jane the sack. "Here you go."

"Thanks." Mac grabbed the card and Jane's hand. They strode out the door quickly. "I guess it's going to be like that from now on."

"Like I'm in a fishbowl and everybody's suddenly got the urge to stare at the weird fish?"

Mac squeezed her hand once before letting go. "Not weird, Jane. Intriguing. You're a mystery here, that's all. We'll run the news spots a few days and if no one steps up with information, we'll take another route. You won't enjoy your celebrity too long."

"Celebrity? More like freak show."

Mac shook his head. There was nothing freaky about Jane. Although she found herself in a precarious situation, she'd held up remarkably well, despite the meltdown she'd had last night. She was a strong woman, Mac surmised, and someone who certainly knew how to put herself together. He wasn't an expert, but he'd waited and watched as she tried on clothes, picking out colors that emphasized her pretty complexion and showed off her flawless figure.

She had class, he'd give her that, and a good sense of style. Even though the highly anticipated and newly built Winchester Mall couldn't compare with big city shopping centers, so far Jane had managed to pick out the right clothes to suit her personality.

Unfortunately for Mac, she looked just as sexy in

them. It didn't matter that the clothes were her correct size and there wasn't a designer label to be had; Jane still looked like a million bucks.

"Where to now?" she asked.

Mac glanced down at her black leather boots. "C'mon. We've got to get you some decent shoes. Summer's just around the corner."

"I'm not ungrateful, but Lizzie's shoes hurt my feet. They are just a little small for me."

They strode toward a store called the Shoe Salon, a small intimate shop that carried nothing but finely detailed women's shoes, the displays themselves nearly a work of art. Mac figured Jane wasn't the department store type. And he also figured she'd be glad to get into something less confining. "I bet those boots can't be any more comfortable than Lizzie's shoes," Mac said.

"Actually, my boots are the most comfortable shoes I own. They're from a little town in Italy. The shoemaker only makes two pairs a month. He makes a mold of your feet and customizes accordingly."

Mac halted abruptly. "What?"

Jane continued walking. "I said, the shoemaker makes only two—"

She stopped and turned to him, her eyes rounding in complete surprise. She stared at Mac for a moment as realization dawned. "Oh my God." She dropped her shiny black bag right where she stood. "Mac, I remembered something," she whispered. Then she repeated, louder this time, her face breaking out in a big smile, "I remembered something."

She rushed into his arms, surprising him once again. "Oh, Mac."

Her joy was contagious. He held her a moment, squeezing his eyes shut and relishing the brief contact.

She pulled away quickly and grinned. "This is good."

"Very good. What else do you remember? The shoe-maker's name? The town in Italy? When did you get the boots? Were they a gift?"

Jane smiled again, shaking her head. "I don't know any of that. I can't recall anything else, but this is a good sign, isn't it? Should we call Dr. Quarles and let him know? Maybe there's something I can do to help my memory along now."

"Not a bad idea. We'll give him a call later."

"Oh, Mac." Jane fell into his arms again. She pressed her head to his chest and he took her in, holding her tight. They stood between Trixie's Toys and Fashion Fare in the middle of the mall, like two teenagers crazy about each other. "Thank you."

She looked up and kissed his cheek.

"What's that for?" he asked, guarding his heart from the unwelcome sense of loss he experienced in that one moment, when he thought Jane might have regained her full memory.

"For being here. For helping me. For giving me your support."

"It's my—"

A flicker of disappointment crossed Jane's face.

"Pleasure. It's my pleasure, Jane."

She smiled again, big and wide, and Mac nudged his

misgivings away. True, she was his case and it was his job to help her, but he finally admitted to himself that he'd do everything in his power to help Jane, whether or not it was his job.

The thought unsettled him. Shook him to the core.

The woman had gotten under his skin.

Tonight, tomorrow or the next day, she might regain her full memory. Then she'd be gone.

"I feel so safe when you hold me, Mac. Like everything's going to be all right."

Mac felt just the opposite. When he held Jane, he felt like nothing in his life would ever be the same.

She pulled away, grabbed his hand and tugged. "Come on, you have summer shoes to buy me."

Jane spread out her new clothes on the bed, arranging the blouses and slacks, the jeans and shorts, making outfits, mixing and matching. She'd been happy with her purchases, realizing that with one week's worth of clothes, she could actually put together nearly a month's wardrobe. All in all, she'd done a decent job. And she hadn't cleaned Mac out, either. She'd been prudent, checking price tags, making sure that she could justify the cost of each piece.

"Wow!" Lizzie knocked on the open door, then came bounding into the room, her soft brown gaze lit with pleasure as she scanned Jane's clothes. "Would you look at all this! These are great, Jane. I love the raspberry outfit. It'll look great with your hair and eyes."

Jane couldn't help smiling. "It was fun, and so sweet of Mac. You both have been so kind."

Lizzie flipped over a price tag, then gave Jane a look of admiration. "Great deal. Did this blouse come in other colors?"

"About five others."

Lizzie smiled. "Mac loved it, you know."

Puzzled, Jane frowned. "The blouse?"

"No, silly. Taking you shopping."

She blinked and her voice rose slightly. "He told you that?"

Lizzie shook her head and wispy auburn bangs fell into her eyes. "Big brother would never admit to actually enjoying a shopping trip. But," she said, looking deeply into Jane's eyes, "he didn't complain. Not once. I think my brother likes you."

Jane's face warmed considerably and she knew a flush of rosy color reached her cheeks. She felt obliged to comment. "He's a nice man," she murmured, though she could describe Mac in much more accurate ways. Strong and steady. Protective yet guarded. Dependable. Commanding. And, oh yeah, sexy as sin. He had a way of looking at her lately that made goose bumps erupt on her arms, and when he held her close, simmering heat spread throughout Jane's entire body.

"That's it? You think he's *nice?*" Lizzie stacked some of Jane's clothes on top of each other and made room for herself on the bed. She sat down, crossed her legs and leaned back, bracing her palms behind her.

"Yes, I do." Jane lifted a white, sleeveless summer dress and put it on a hanger. It was a last-minute purchase, an item Mac had encouraged her to buy. She'd need at least one dress, she figured, so she hadn't argued about it. She hung up the dress in the closet, then turned. "What are you getting at?"

Lizzie shot her a mischievous smile. "Mac needs a woman in his life."

"Oh, Lizzie. And you think it's going to be me?"

"You like him, Jane. I can see how you look at him."

"Of course I like him. He saved my life, took me in." With a sweep of her hands, she gestured to the clothes on the bed. "He put clothes on my back. I'm grateful to you and Mac, but there's no future for us, I'm afraid. I don't know who I am. Mac is right to guard himself from the likes of me."

"So you don't think he's a great guy?"

"Lizzie, Mac is a great guy and he certainly doesn't need you matchmaking for him," she said softly. "So why are you? And what about your own love life?"

She let out a deep, gloomy sigh. "What love life?"

Jane sat down next to her. "What about Deputy Brody?"

Lizzie shrugged, but her eyes lit just at the mention of his name.

"Tell me," Jane said gently. "I'd love to help."

"It's just that… I think he's afraid of what Mac might say."

"Lizzie, you're a grown woman and you have a right to make your own choices in life. Besides, Lyle Brody is a decent man, from what I've seen of him. Why would Mac object?"

Again, Lizzie shrugged. "It's complicated." She searched Jane's face for a moment, as if deciding whether to confide in her. "I want to see Mac happy, for one. He deserves it. He's been alone too long and, well, I'd feel like I'd be abandoning him. Sure, he's overbearing at times and we butt heads on occasion, but I know in my heart that he'd give his life for me. He's a great brother."

Jane understood Lizzie's loyalty, to a point. And while she thought it wonderful that Lizzie and Mac shared such a special bond, she wondered about her own life. Did she have a brother somewhere searching for her? Was there anyone out there willing to lay down his life for her? It was moments like this when Jane felt so alone, so lost. The hollowness inside ate at her at times, until she had to mentally obliterate those feelings of despair before they took her down.

Jane had hope now. She'd remembered something today. It had to be just a matter of time before her memory returned. She clung desperately to that hope. She'd tried to speak with Dr. Quarles this afternoon, but he wasn't in his office. Tomorrow she'd make an appointment to see him.

"Mac wants you happy, Lizzie. I'd bet my last dollar on it." Then she grinned. "If I had one, that is."

Lizzie smiled too, only briefly. "But there's more, Jane. And I'm not sure Mac would appreciate me talking about this."

"I understand," she said, though she was dying to know what else Lizzie had to say.

"Of course, if you forced it out of me, then I couldn't be blamed."

Jane grinned again, realizing why Lizzie was a favorite among her students at Winchester High. She was so childlike in her own way, but still a woman with needs and desires that shouldn't be ignored. Lizzie deserved to have a life of her own. She deserved a man to love, a home and a family. Jane had a hard time believing that Mac would deny her those pleasures.

"I'm officially forcing it out of you. I'll take all blame. I'm not giving you a choice." She winked and nodded.

"Okay," Lizzie said, picking up the shoe box holding Jane's new, strappy tan sandals. She lifted the lid off, then replaced it. "Ask me about Lyle."

"Why doesn't Mac want you to see Lyle Brody?"

"Well, because you're forcing me, I'll tell you. Mac was married to Lyle's sister, Brenda Lee."

The air rushed out of Jane's lungs. She felt empty, deflated, and she couldn't quite understand why. She'd known that Mac had been married once, but speaking about it, giving the woman a name, made it all seem so real. Jane had no right to feel even the slightest bit of jealousy, but she did, and the fingers of that emotion inched up her spine in a slow crawl. "Oh my."

Lizzie breathed deeply and nodded. "You see now. The breakup wasn't pretty, and of course, Lyle's just as protective of his sister as Mac is of me. They respect each other professionally, but Lyle is Mac's ex-brother-in-law. Makes it kind of tricky, doesn't it?"

"And you're in love with Lyle, aren't you?"

"I think I could be, Jane. But we haven't been able to explore the possibilities."

Sensations washed over Jane as she thought about

Mac and his marriage to Lyle's sister. She had a burning desire to learn about his failed marriage and couldn't resist prying, just a little. "So what happened with Brenda Lee?"

"Oh, she and Mac never really were suited for each other. Once they married, Brenda Lee thought she could change him. She wanted to leave Winchester in the dust and she thought she could convince Mac to take her away from here. Mac struggled with it for a long time, but he couldn't change who he was. She never got that Mac was a small-town sheriff, and he'd always be one. Mac likes his life, this town, his job. He never expected that she'd demand such drastic changes. Mac couldn't stop being Mac, not even to save his marriage."

"Wow."

"Yeah, but Brenda Lee got what she wanted. She lives in New York now, remarried, with two children."

"So, you'd feel disloyal to Mac on both fronts, if you got involved with Lyle."

"Yes, that's so true. When you entered the picture and I saw how Mac reacted to you, I can't tell you the sense of relief I felt. Mac hasn't been interested—I mean seriously interested—in a woman in a long time."

"He keeps telling me that he's not, Lizzie. I hate to break the bad news to you, but Mac sees me as his responsibility, nothing more."

"Right, and the sun doesn't set in the west every afternoon."

Flustered, Jane didn't know what to say.

"My brother doesn't invite women into our home,

whether or not she has amnesia. He doesn't take her shopping and then buy her gifts if he's not interested." Lizzie reached into the pocket of her blouse and pulled out a gold box. "He wanted me to give this to you."

Jane accepted the gilded box Lizzie shoved her way, staring at her with total surprise.

"Well, open it. I'm dying to see what it is."

Slowly, with deft fingers, Jane pried open the box. "Oh," she said softly, as tears pooled in her eyes. She pulled out a set of matching, stamped silver earrings, necklace and bracelet—large round hoops connected by smaller links. "I took one long look at these in the window while we were shopping. I didn't think Mac noticed. I didn't want him to notice, Lizzie. I couldn't possibly expect him to buy me jewelry."

"But he did."

"Yes, he did," Jane said quietly, hugging the box to her chest and hard-pressed to name all of the warm emotions whirling by. "Why didn't he give them to me himself?"

Lizzie's smile widened. "Probably because he couldn't take seeing that look in your eyes. You've nearly got me teared up, too."

"I don't know what to say."

"Just do me a favor? When you thank him, don't make a huge deal about it. Mac's not into big thank-yous. It's enough that he sees you wearing them."

"I'm not sure I should even accept them, Lizzie."

"They didn't break his bank account, Jane. And you'd hurt his feelings, big time, if you sent them back."

Jane fingered the necklace, playing with the hoops

and admiring the fine details. Of all the expensive jewelry she'd seen today, stealing glances in shop windows, this simple silver set had impressed her most. And Mac had picked up on that.

Small wonder. He had great investigative skills and good instincts.

"On second thought, I couldn't possibly send them back. Help me put them on?" She handed the necklace to Lizzie.

"Sure, but on one condition. When I get back from my trip, you'll help me tackle a whole new wardrobe. I need to go on a shopping spree of my own."

"I'd love to, Lizzie. Sounds like fun. But where are you going?"

"North Carolina. My best friend, Caitlin, is delivering her baby earlier than expected. And her husband, Joe, is on a mission overseas. The marines won't send him home anytime soon. I'm going to be her birth partner and the baby's godmother."

"That's wonderful. How long will you be gone?"

Lizzie bounded up from the bed to fasten the necklace around Jane's neck. "I'm leaving on Sunday and I'll be gone less than a week. But long enough for you and Mac to figure out where you stand."

Jane stood there, wearing the jewelry Mac had given her, shaking her head at Lizzie. "Mac's going to think you're matchmaking."

"It's not my fault that Caitlin had some complications. They're taking the baby early, by caesarean section. I can't let my friend down. A promise is a promise, and I'm thrilled to be a part of the birth." She smiled, showing a beautiful set of white teeth, so much like her brother's. "But I have to admit," she added, cocking her head, "the timing couldn't be more perfect."

Six

Jane stood at the back door, debating about going into Mac's garage this morning. She'd heard him exit the kitchen, and berated herself for not rising earlier to catch him during breakfast. He hadn't come home for dinner last night after their shopping trip, Lizzie explaining that he'd been called into the sheriff's station for an emergency. And Jane had yet to thank him for his generous gift.

She wore the jewelry today, the silver pieces setting off her new sleeveless lilac blouse and lightweight black slacks very nicely. It completed the outfit, making her feel more put together than she had all week. The weather had warmed up considerably, the Colorado summer taking hold, and Jane's new clothes lent her the cool comfort she needed. She'd even put her hair up in a ponytail, and wondered if that was something she'd been inclined to do. Was she the tomboyish, ponytail type of woman? She didn't know, but right now having her hair up brought a cooling breeze to her neck and throat. Something she figured she'd need, if Mac were working out in his gym as she suspected.

She heaved a heavy sigh and strode toward the garage. She knew one thing about herself—her thank-yous couldn't wait. But just as a precaution, instead of entering the garage, she decided to steal a quick peek through the window. She saw no sign of Mac in there and didn't know if she was relieved or disappointed. Just as she began to turn away, his voice boomed in her ear.

"Looking for me?"

She whirled around and found him leaning against the fence post, sipping from his water bottle. His bronzed chest glistened under the Colorado sun, and once again he wore nothing but his sweatpants and a white towel draped around his neck.

"Oh, Mac. Yes, I was. I…didn't want to interrupt your workout."

"I'm through," he said, taking a last sip from his bottle. He set it on the post and approached her.

It was all Jane could do to keep from backing away. Mac stared at her in a way that made her heart race, her nerves jangle and her lips pucker, among other parts of her anatomy. She saw his gaze flicker to her throat, taking in the necklace, then the bracelet and finally catching the gleam of the hoop earrings she wore.

"You look pretty," he said as he came to stand before her.

She blushed, swallowing hard. Her hand instinctively reached for the necklace. It was the first time Mac had paid her a direct, unabashed compliment. "Oh, um, that's why I came out here. To thank you. I love the jewelry, but then you must have known that."

He nodded, and Jane didn't gush with thanks, keeping in mind what Lizzie had told her. "It was a nice surprise."

"Jane," Mac began, staring into her eyes. Her pulse escalated until she thought she'd faint. She waited for him to continue, but when he only stared, she realized it was the first time she'd seen him at a loss for words. She didn't know what to make of it.

"Did you want something?"

He lifted one corner of his mouth, not in a smile as she knew it, but more a sardonic expression. "Not a good question to ask of a man who wants…"

"Wants? What do you want, Mac?"

As if catching himself for mistakenly revealing a real, undisguised emotion, Mac started to retreat. Jane grabbed both ends of the towel hugging his neck and tugged, refusing to let him go.

She stood toe to toe with him, looking up into his handsome face.

His eyes darkened to nearly black. Then his gaze focused on her mouth.

Swamped with heat, pulsating with desire, Jane parted her lips.

Mac groaned, closing his eyes briefly.

"What do you want?" she asked again, this time as softly as a summer wind.

"Not here," he said enigmatically, puzzling Jane even more. Then he took her hand, tugged her along with him into the garage and pressed her up against the wall. Bracing his hands on either side of her, trapping her, he lowered his mouth on hers for a deep, long, openmouthed kiss.

Jane moaned, sighing with pleasure. She hadn't expected this—not anything like this—but she wasn't complaining. Though it was totally insane, she couldn't deny Mac this kiss, or anything else he might want.

She stroked his smooth, slick skin, running her hands up and down his chest, curling her fingers into the mass of curling hairs. He was firm and well muscled, and Jane couldn't get enough of Sheriff Mac Riggs. Her hands slid over him again and again, until he, too, couldn't get enough. He pressed his body closer, his tight, hard erection rubbing her belly. Jane thought she'd die from the sensations.

"Oh, Mac," she breathed, willing him to take everything he wanted. And somehow, a moment later, Jane's blouse was undone, and Mac was there, sliding his hands inside, caressing her sensitive flesh.

He flicked his thumbs over her nipples, back and forth, heightening her pleasure until she wanted to scream out. Mac kissed her again and again, trailing his lips down her throat, licking her skin until the anticipation grew too much. Jane arched for him, offering herself, and he bent his head to take her inside his mouth, hot and moist and slick.

"You're so damn perfect," he whispered in a husky voice, lifting up to kiss her again. "I want all of you, honey."

Jane searched his gaze, finding desire there, a stark, dark desperation in his eyes. She felt the same, and nodded as much. She wanted Mac to make love to her, to find a place inside her and stay until both of them were sated and spent and exhausted. She wanted that connection. To feel. To belong. She wanted all that. And only with Mac.

He moved her along with him, without breaking the connection until he lowered her down onto his workout bench. Within a second his body covered hers, and she noted how careful he was, how much he held back so as not to crush her.

He moved slowly, taking his time now, kissing her, stroking her, his body rubbing hers in all the right places. She ached for him. Everything inside her cried out for completion with this man.

And when he finally reached for the zipper of her slacks, Jane sucked in her breath, making it easier for him.

Bells rang.

At first Jane thought it was a school bell. Or the clanging of a fire truck.

Mac stopped midway with her zipper.

He listened.

Then he sat up, and she felt the immediate loss.

"What is it?" she asked.

"My cell phone, Jane. Something's up. Either at the station or with Lizzie."

Yet he allowed the ringing to continue. He glanced down at her, and she felt suddenly exposed and vulnerable. But his eyes held hers, telling her in unspoken words that it was okay. And with that one look he vanquished any embarrassment she might have had.

He reached for her hand, lifted her to an upright position on the workout bench and sighed. "Jane, it's a good thing the phone rang."

She didn't agree.

"I didn't even think about a condom."

Jane buttoned her blouse, and he watched until she was fully dressed again. She sensed his retreat, the backlash of his actions to follow.

"This is crazy," he said, standing now, admonishing himself. Mac wasn't a man to lose control, and Jane figured he'd be blaming himself for this. "I wasn't thinking, period. How are you going to forgive me?"

She stood then, mustering her courage and tamping down her anger. "Shut up, Mac."

He snapped his head up. "What?"

"Don't you dare apologize to me. I'm a big girl, fully capable of making decisions for myself." Jane turned away so he wouldn't see her distress. "Don't you have to see about that phone call?"

"Jane?"

"Just go, Mac," she said forcefully. Then more softly, she repeated, "Just go."

"Are you all right?"

Jane wanted to scream "No!" She wasn't all right. Nothing had been right since she lost her memory. But for a few brief moments this morning, she'd thought that maybe everything would be all right. With Mac. And her.

"I'm fine."

Mac lifted the cell phone from the worktable and glanced at the number. "It's the station."

"So, call them back."

He glanced over at her, standing there by his workout bench, the place where both of their lives might have changed this morning. "I'm—"

"Don't say it, Mac. I'm warning you."

He actually smiled, as if her tone amused him, then turned to make his phone call.

Jane bounded out of the garage, filled with enough emotions to sink a cruise liner. She needed out of here, fast.

And that was exactly what she decided to do.

Leave.

Mac stepped out of the shower, dried off quickly and dressed. He had to get to the station as soon as possible, and he had to speak with Jane. The news he'd gotten involved her, but Mac wasn't too thrilled to have to spend any more time with her this morning. Hell, what had he been thinking earlier, in the garage? He'd almost made love to her like some smitten, hormone-crazed teen without the sense God had given him.

It wasn't like Mac to lose control like that. He'd prided himself on his rationality and good judgment. He'd been alone a long time, he told himself. And he was sexually attracted to Jane.

What living, breathing man wouldn't be?

But he'd thought he could manage having her live under his roof. After all, they had Lizzie as a chaperone. The thought that he *needed* a chaperone around Jane made him nuts. Where had all his willpower gone?

He'd like to turn his baby sister over his knee just thinking about her obvious ploy to shove Jane at him every chance she could. Lizzie had *never* been out of the house this much. She'd never had "meetings" or "appointments" in the evenings that kept her out late.

As soon as Jane had arrived on the scene, his sister had made herself scarce.

Mac made a mental note to read her the riot act the next time they were alone. Lizzie didn't know she was playing with fire. Mac had already been burned once, and though he'd gotten over the searing pain a long time ago, he wasn't stupid enough to jump into the flames again. And Lizzie's latest news, about leaving on Sunday to spend nearly a week with Caitlin, wasn't what he wanted to hear.

"Babies come when they want," Lizzie had said, "and I can't help it if this one is coming early. Caitlin had some complications and she needs a C-section. You know, darn well I promised I'd be there, Mac."

Yeah, Mac had known, but he hadn't planned on being left entirely alone with Jane for all that time. Still, he couldn't really fault Lizzie on that one, but he didn't have to like it.

He'd made himself a personal vow to keep a safe distance from Jane, but that wasn't easy when he spent time with her during the day for duty's sake, and nights with her at home. Hell, there was no use starting up something with a woman who was here only temporarily. He berated himself again for not exercising more caution when it came to Jane.

But when he'd seen her today, looking bright and pretty in her new clothes, wearing the jewelry he thought she'd deserved, something inside him had snapped. A possessive, almost carnal urge had taken hold. The jewelry had glistened on her skin, catching the light and beaming at him, and Mac had found himself at a loss. He'd only wanted one thing.

Jane.

"And look where that got you, buddy," he said ruefully.

He managed to stop himself in time, but if his phone hadn't chimed, ringing loud enough to wake the dead, would he have had the good sense to call a halt to making love to her?

"You only managed to confuse her even more," he said quietly as he stepped out of his bedroom. He knew that the last thing Jane needed in her life was more chaos and uncertainty. And he also knew he'd blown it with her in a major way. He didn't think he would ever forget that look of hurt and disappointment on her face when he'd come to his senses. Hell, he'd been damn disappointed, too. But he'd never be able to convince Jane of that. She wasn't too happy with him right now, but he had to face her, to tell her the news he'd received this morning.

"Jane," he called out, walking through all the rooms in his house. An eerie silence followed.

He heaved a sigh and went searching. Five minutes

later, after checking and rechecking the house and grounds, Mac got in his patrol car and slammed the door. His heart beat like crazy as he wondered where she was. The lawman in him hated the fact that because of the way he'd found her—alone, abandoned on that ridge—he hadn't really ruled out foul play. Had someone come searching for her? Had someone meant her harm?

It wasn't like Jane to leave the house so abruptly. Mac hated the route his mind had taken. He pressed the gas pedal and took off slowly, scouring the streets of Winchester in hopes of finding a gorgeous blonde with a hot temper.

When he finally found her, he had to tamp down his own raging temper, allowing himself one brief moment of relief. He spotted her on the main street of town, speaking to—no, actually laughing with—Lyle Brody. If he recalled correctly, this was his deputy's day off, and the fact that he wore jeans and a blue plaid shirt verified Mac's assumption. They stood in front of Tyler's Market, Lyle shifting a bag of groceries in his arms.

Mac parked the car ten yards down the street and waited. When neither looked his way, he counted to ten, a precaution he'd learned to take whenever he felt the urge to do something impulsive, then got out of his car.

He leaned against the passenger side door and waited, arms folded.

Whether Jane didn't see him or just refused to acknowledge him, he couldn't be sure. After another round of counting to ten, he approached, keeping his stride and his demeanor casual.

"Morning." He spoke to Lyle.

Both seemed truly surprised to see him standing there, which only added to his irritation. What had been so dang interesting that the two had blotted out the rest of the world?

"Hey, Sheriff," Lyle said, straightening up and wiping the grin from his face. "Look who I bumped into. Jane and I were—"

"I'm here on official business. I need to speak with Jane," Mac interrupted. It grated on his nerves, seeing the two of them so chummy.

"Sure thing. I'd better get these groceries put up." Lyle cast Jane a quick smile. "Nice seeing you again."

"Same here, Lyle. Remember what I said."

Lyle nodded, darting a glance at Mac, and once again Mac wondered what the hell was up. "Will do. See you around."

Jane folded her arms across her middle and stood ramrod still. "Well, that was rude."

"What's rude, Jane, is leaving the house without telling me where you were going."

"I went for a walk, Mac. That's all. No great mystery here. Sometimes I need to get out and clear my head."

Mac figured it was more than that. Both had been left anxious and unnerved by what had happened in the garage this morning. And in Mac's case, filled with sexual energy that he had a damn hard time shutting down. "Next time, leave a note. I'm still responsible for you."

Jane shook her head. "Listen—"

"I have news about your case," he said, avoiding

what was certain to be an argument coming. "Take a drive with me."

"News? About me?" Jane's expression changed, her blond brows lifting and her blue eyes gleaming with hope. At the very least he had managed to get her out of her sour mood. He only hoped that once he took her to the scene, she would remember something. Part of him wanted Jane to regain her memory and leave Winchester for good, while the other part struggled with the idea of her leaving.

When he'd found her gone this morning, he'd worried about her for professional reasons, but he'd also worried about her for personal ones. And those sentiments could get a man like him in big trouble.

"C'mon." Mac began walking toward his patrol car. "They're waiting. I'll fill you in on the drive out of town."

"So this is it," Mac said, parking the car on the bank of Cascade Lake. "Looks like our timing is perfect."

Jane glanced around, her nerves frazzled from all that had happened this morning. Now maybe she had a chance, a clue as to her identity, and though Mac had warned her on the way up here not to get too hopeful, she couldn't quite help it. "It's beautiful," she said, staring out onto the lake. Deep blue waters glistened under the Colorado sun, tall trees in springtime hues lined the far shore and the last vestiges of winter snow tipped glorious Pike's Peak in the background.

"There's a lot of history here," Mac said. "This was one of the first places to be settled in the West."

But the grind of heavy machinery marred the moment, and both she and Mac turned their heads toward the sound.

"Looks like a red Mustang."

A team of local lawman stood on the sidelines as the car was dragged out of the lake.

They exited the patrol car, Mac coming around to stand beside her. "All you have to do is take a look. See if it sparks your memory in any way. It's a long shot at best, Jane. But, since we believe you were driving a car that we have yet to find, this could make sense. We've found two other cars this way, stripped of any identity, no registration, no license plates, but we've managed to find one of the owners."

"Were the cars stolen?"

"Yeah, we think it's nothing more than joyriders, since they don't strip the cars for parts. We have an idea about who's doing it, but what we don't have is proof."

"So, you think that someone might have stolen the car I'd been driving?"

Mac shrugged. "It's a possibility. Let's get closer to take a better look."

Jane reached the vehicle, with Mac standing right beside her. She stared at the Mustang, which was drenched, and coated with debris from being at the bottom of the lake. She looked long and hard, then shook her head. "Nothing comes to mind, Mac. I don't think I've ever seen this car before."

Mac pressed the small of her back and urged her forward. "Take a look inside."

She did. She glanced inside to see a soaked, yet barren interior, devoid of any signs that might give her a clue. She shook her head again.

"We still have the trunk. One of the cars we found like this had nothing inside to help us out, but the other did. We found a few items along with a grocery receipt lying on the floor of the trunk. From that, we were able to locate the owner. They'll tow the car in and check the trunk at the station."

"When were the other cars found?" she asked.

"This month. The investigators believe that there's a gang of teenagers out for some fun. Troublemakers mostly, and not the kind of kids you'd want to have around. We'll find them. It's only a matter of time."

Jane faced the car once more, studying it with intensity. Again, she shook her head slowly, not seeing or feeling what she'd hoped. "I don't think this is my car, Mac."

"Probably not, but we'll find out for sure once the trunk is opened. If it is yours, there might be luggage or other identifying items in there. We can rule out the other car we found, since it showed up well before you landed in Winchester."

"What now?"

"Give me a minute. I have to speak with Sergeant Meeker with the Pueblo PD."

"Okay."

Jane watched Mac head toward the hub of lawmen huddled together at the rear of the Mustang. She stared out onto the lake, breathing in fresh, crisp air, enjoying the scenery once again and allowing the calm serenity to dip inside and soothe her nerves. She couldn't recall ever having seen such a lovely spot, not that she would, of course. But Cascade Lake was something special. The surrounding wildflowers in lavender, blue, pink and yellow made a colorful array against the water. She walked a little along the bank, away from the crime scene. She thought she'd like to come here again one day, when there wasn't so much tumult in her life. She'd like to simply sit by the water's edge and drink in the view.

"Jane?"

She turned to find Mac behind her, watching her with those dark, knowing eyes.

"Want to take a walk?"

She nodded.

They began to stroll along the shore, both deep in thought. Finally, when a large grouping of rocks prevented them from going any farther, they stopped. "Let's sit for a while," Mac said.

They found a long flat boulder and sat down next to each other. "I've got good memories of this place," he said quietly as he gazed across the expanse of the lake. "Used to come down here and skip rocks when I was a kid. Had my first kiss here, too, when I was twelve."

Jane laughed. "Twelve?" Mac lifted his lips, the brilliance of his seldom-seen smile tugging at Jane. "Seems you were an early learner."

"Bungled my way through, and both of us nearly landed facedown in the lake. Man, I was so nervous."

"But determined."

Mac nodded. "Always."

"And was she your girl from then on out?"

"You kidding? She dumped me the next day," Mac said, chuckling. "Can't say as I blame her."

Jane imagined Mac as a young, eager boy, long and lanky and probably awkward as heck trying to impress a young girl. He certainly had improved his skills since then. Jane had been swept away this morning by Mac's "skill" and found him passionate, caring and thoughtful. She'd been overwhelmed by desire, and she doubted she'd ever met a man in her life that could measure up to him.

Even though she didn't know about her life, she felt sure in her heart that no man could possibly make her feel the way Mac did.

Mac's smile faded then and he turned to meet her eyes. "About this morning, Jane—"

She put up a hand. "Don't."

"I'm not apologizing," he said quickly. "But I am taking responsibility. I should have known better. It was more than an innocent kiss and we both know where we were heading."

Jane nodded, unwilling to sugarcoat what had happened this morning. Mac was right—if that phone call hadn't broken the spell, they would have made love, right there on the workout bench and who knows where else. It was that intense. That powerful.

"But it can't happen, Jane. You don't know your circumstances, and until you do…"

"What, Mac? There are never any guarantees in life."

"I know that," he said with a long, laborious sigh.

"But I got involved with a woman once who didn't know herself. She thought she could be content with life as it was, but once we married, nothing was enough for her. *I* wasn't enough for her. We'd be foolish to think that your life, your *real* life, won't take precedence over anything you might find here with me."

"No, I can't guarantee that. I know what you're saying is true, Mac. But I have little to go on here. I only know what I feel."

Mac smiled broadly and her heart flipped over itself again. "I know what I feel, too."

"And what's that?" Jane asked, her heart pounding hard.

He hesitated a few seconds, then said, with clear honest eyes, "I want you."

Warmth spread throughout her body, and Jane realized she had to be content with that knowledge. She wouldn't press Mac. He was trying darn hard to be reasonable, rational and responsible.

The rat.

"I know about your wife, Mac. Lizzie sort of filled me in."

He scowled.

"Don't be angry with her. She only wants your happiness."

"She's a pill."

Jane laughed, and the sound echoed against the wall of trees surrounding the lake. "She's a sweetheart."

Mac granted her half a smile. "That, too." Then he took a long, drawn-out breath. "Listen, you know Lizzie is leaving on Sunday. It's not what I had planned when I invited you to stay with us. We're going to be alone, and if you don't want to—"

"Do you want me to leave?" Jane asked, point-blank. Heart racing, she had to know the answer. She didn't want to overstay her welcome, and if Mac thought her leaving would make his life easier, then she'd go. Earlier this morning she'd called Dr. Quarles to make an appointment, and once again, he had been gracious to offer her an open-ended invitation to his hospitality.

"No," Mac stated immediately. "I was only asking for your sake. Not mine."

"If it makes you feel any better, I won't be home all that much. Lizzie helped me get a job at Touched with Love. I'll be volunteering at the bookstore every day." She beamed him a smile. Once she'd finalized the arrangements today, the thought really took hold. She couldn't wait to get started and to do something productive with her life. "Rory assured me that my working there wouldn't interfere with our investigation. Anytime you need me I can be available. And in between times I'll be helping him out over there."

"Lizzie arranged that for you?"

She nodded. "Yes, she's very friendly with Rory Holcomb. Seems his grandchildren have been in her classes, all six of them. And it's close enough for me to walk to work and back."

Mac's expression faltered. "It's not that close to home, Jane. I'd rather you didn't work at night."

"Oh, so you want me home nights. Alone. With you?"

Mac pursed his lips, then shook his head in resignation. "All right. You've made your point. But I'll be picking you up from the shop when you do work nights. And that's *not* negotiable."

"It's a deal. I can't wait to get started," Jane said with a happy sigh. "It's the one positive thing I have to look forward to."

"Is that where you went this morning?"

"Yes, I'd heard his used book store was charming. I wanted to meet Rory in person and see his place."

"And you failed to tell me. Made me worry like crazy."

Jane turned her head to look him in the eyes. "You worried?"

Mac scratched his head and rose abruptly, refusing to answer. "I've got to get back to work."

Jane walked back to the car with him, struggling with her thoughts. She'd thought she'd angered Mac by taking off without his permission. She thought it more an ego thing on his part. She hadn't thought about him worrying about her. Worrying meant caring. And caring led to other things.

After this morning she knew Mac wanted her. But that had been sexual. He'd been attracted to her physically. But Jane hadn't thought past that. She hadn't thought he actually cared for her. Not in the personal, intimate way a man cares for a woman.

She was his responsibility. Hadn't he told her that a dozen times? He felt duty-bound to help her.

Jane picked up her pace and reached the patrol car before Mac. She got in, slamming the door and staring straight ahead. She couldn't possibly afford to think that Mac actually cared for her. It would be dangerous to believe so. Yet her heart burned with the thought.

Putting distance between them would be the wisest route to take. Jane had the means now, by working long hours at the bookstore. She planned on staying far out of Mac's reach.

His heart wasn't the only one that could get broken.

And in her vulnerable state, Jane knew she would shatter to pieces if that happened.

Seven

The next morning Jane stepped into Touched with Love and a great sense of belonging swept over her. She breathed in the musky scent of yellowed pages turned by loving hands, of aged bindings holding leaves together by vintage strength, and of softly worn leather sofas placed in a semicircle in one corner of the bookstore. The "reading cove," as Rory had affectionately called it, was a place for old and young alike to gather. In the afternoons, children clustered on the sofas and listened as Rory read them their favorite tales. The evenings were shared by the Women of Winchester, a historical reading group, as well as the Book Banterers, an eclectic group who delved into elements of the paranormal.

All in all, Jane felt welcome here. She fit in somehow,

and a sweet, sweeping sensation of rightness filled her. Not even the softly played country tunes wafting in the air could stifle these newfound impressions of belonging. She'd come to know the likes of Toby and Martina, Kenny and Shania, George and Tim. Living in the Riggs household, she hadn't had a choice. Good thing the rock and twang had seeped into her soul. She'd caught herself toe tapping to the tunes often enough.

She had to admit she enjoyed listening to KWIN, and all the antics of the radio station's disc jockeys. Though originally she'd been stunned, she had eventually gotten accustomed to hearing her description play on air, as well. "The young blond woman with blue eyes, an amnesia victim found on the outskirts of town. If anyone has information regarding Winchester's own Jane Doe, please contact the Winchester County Sheriff's Department."

"Morning," Rory said, looking up from a stack of paperbacks ready to be shelved. "You're here bright and early."

"Hello, Rory. I couldn't wait to get started."

"We're not officially open for half an hour. I was just about to have a cup of coffee and a doughnut. Marietta bakes them up fresh every morning. She brings me a batch for my customers. It'd be nice to have someone to share them with. Come, let's sit awhile. I don't expect a crowd until later in the day."

"I'd love to."

After two cups of coffee and a sugar doughnut, Jane set about her work. She organized a stack of mysteries, alphabetizing them, but not without reading their back cover blurbs and perusing their first pages. The feel of the books, the print on the page all seemed so familiar to her, yet she had no real recollection, no hint as to why. All she knew was that she liked being here, and it felt darn good finally being able to do something productive.

The day flew by. She worked alongside Rory, and when he had to leave the shop for an hour, he entrusted it to her care. He brought them both back lunch, and in between helping customers, they stuffed down their sandwiches.

Rory turned over the children's reading hour to her, introducing Jane to the children as his new "reading buddy." Rory had paired up the children, teaming them so that when they had an opportunity to read, they could work out the tougher words together. Sometimes Jane would read a story, and sometimes the children would read one to her.

"Aren't you getting hungry?"

"A little," Jane answered automatically. Her head down, she was focused intently on a compelling thriller she hadn't been able to shelve just yet. When she glanced up, she found Mac leaning beside her in the mystery section, watching her with interest.

"Oh, hi," she said lamely, amazed at how his presence always seemed to fluster her lately, and now his scent, that fresh lime aftershave, mixed with his own essence, remained with her even after he'd stalked off somewhere. "What are you doing here?"

"It's almost eight. Rory left hours ago. His oldest grandchild, Jimmy, is working the cash register now, readying to close up."

"Oh," Jane said, remembering that she'd bade farewell earlier. He'd told her to go on home, and Jane had planned to, but she'd gotten involved in the thriller. "I lost track of time."

Mac took the book out of her hand, closing it and eyeing the title. "Good?"

"I couldn't put it down."

"I'm starving," he said. "Let's go eat."

Surprised, Jane followed him to the cash register. "You haven't eaten yet?"

"Nope." He shook his head, and Jane was too dumbfounded to realize that Mac had paid for the book she'd been reading. When he handed it to her with a quick lift of his lips, she blinked.

"Why not?"

He shrugged as he headed for the front door. "I had a late call tonight. You weren't home when I finally got there, so I drove over to pick you up."

Jane finally glanced down at the book in her hands. She reminded herself not to read too much into simple gestures of kindness, but those gestures, coming from the stanch and stubborn sheriff, sent her mind spinning.

Dusk had settled on the horizon and she realized that Mac felt duty bound to pick her up this evening. She abhorred being a complication in his life, and at the same time felt as though it was more than that. Her heart warmed considerably at the notion. She'd tried to stay away today, losing herself in the bookstore and her volunteer work. She'd had a nice day, actually, but nothing compared to being with Mac.

He stood tall, wearing his tan uniform proudly, watching her, and Jane nibbled on her lower lip, staring at her reflection in his silver badge. "I'll make dinner when we get...*home*." Using the word in that context set her mind spinning again. She was beginning to feel that 2785 Crescent Drive was her home. And she had handsome Mac Riggs waiting on dinner for her.

"No need. We're going out. Best place in town."

Jane glanced down at her clothes. She'd known she would work in the bookstore today, shelving, opening cartons and getting down on the floor with little ones to help them pick out books, so she'd worn her old jeans and a nothing-special blouse. "Should I go home to change?"

Mac grinned and placed a hand on her waist, urging her to his car. "Not a chance, Jane. You're dressed exactly right."

"I still say you're chicken, Jane."

She sat at the back end of Mac's Trailblazer in Colorado Chuck's parking lot, dangling her feet and eating an Aspen burger with pickles and tomato out of a cardboard box. Mac opted for a Pike's Peak, a mountainous burger filled with chili and cheese and onions and heaven knows what else, definitely the more dangerous choice. Jane's stomach rumbled at the sight of the monstrous meal.

"Not chicken, just smart." She pointed at his burger. "I hope you have a jar of antacids at home."

"I have a stomach of steel." He took a giant bite of his burger.

Jane couldn't disagree. She'd seen his bare chest, the rippling muscles and hard-packed abs. The image stayed in her head until she shook it free. "You'll need it. If the burger doesn't kill you, the fries surely will."

"Ah, but what a way to go." He popped a fry into his mouth.

Jane smiled, nibbling on her meal while she watched Mac indulge in his. "You sure know how to treat a lady," she teased.

"You ain't seen nothing yet," he bantered back, and it was clear he took no offense in her statement. "You haven't experienced Winchester until you've had one of Colorado Chuck's Pike's Peaks." He shook his head. "Too bad, Jane. You don't know what you're missing."

"Maybe next time. I mean…if I come back here… sometime…ever again."

With his burger halfway to his mouth, Mac stopped to look at her squarely. Their eyes met for a long moment and he let out a long sigh. The fact that Jane would leave Winchester someday, maybe sooner than later, lay like a deep sea of doubt between them.

Jane swallowed the lump in her throat and took a small bite of her burger.

"Do you know how many little towns and villages there are in Italy?" Mac said, finishing his meal and crumpling his napkin. "Hundreds."

"Wow," Jane said, glad Mac changed the subject. She didn't want to think about leaving Winchester, or Mac, anytime soon. But she couldn't wait to regain her memory and find out about herself. She felt stuck between a rock and a hard place, the catch-22 of her situation not lost on her. "I guess I might have known that at one time. So, no luck finding our friendly little Italian shoemaker?"

Mac answered with a shake of his head. "We're not giving up. Would help if we had the cobbler's name, though. Anything else come to mind?"

Jane finished her burger, leaving the fries untouched and finally washing it all down with a strawberry shake. "No, sorry. I've thought about those boots over and over. You've got me dreaming of stiletto heels and black leather, but nothing comes to mind."

Mac nearly choked on his chocolate shake. He sputtered, spraying chocolate onto the asphalt parking lot. "Man, Jane. I think I'll be the one dreaming of stiletto heels and black leather tonight."

Jane punched him playfully on the arm, but the heat of his gaze froze her in action. He wasn't kidding. Desire burned in his dark eyes and her body heated quickly.

One passionate look from the sheriff was all it took to turn Jane's subdued demeanor into a sizzling wreck of nerves.

The remembered feel of his lips on hers, his hands caressing her body, his long lean form atop her on that workout bench yesterday, filled her mind and put an ache in her heart. She grabbed both cardboard boxes, jumped down from the back of the SUV and walked over to the trash, dumping everything inside.

When she turned back around, she found Mac

speaking with a woman, a young, pretty brunette with a curvy body and a proprietary hand on his arm. The woman hadn't wasted any time in approaching Mac as soon as the coast was clear.

Jane hesitated a few seconds, then, with decided assertion, walked right back over to them. "Hi, I'm Jane." She put out her hand.

The taller woman shook it, a quizzical look on her face. "Lola. I'm a…friend of Mac's."

Jane nodded and smiled. "That makes two of us."

Mac sat silently by, watching the exchange, offering nothing.

"Mac and I go back a long way," Lola said, smiling at him. "Don't we, Sheriff?"

He shrugged, sipping his shake. "Guess we do. We were both born and bred in Winchester."

"School chums, then?" Jane asked, though she really didn't enjoy being a part of this conversation. Her heart raced, but a deep sense of dread overshadowed any other sensation she felt at the moment. While half of her cried out with jealous regret, the other half felt heavy, like a lead weight around Mac's neck, pulling him down. Since being found up at Deerlick Canyon, Jane had tied up all Mac's time, taking him away from any personal life he might want to have. She'd been his responsibility, and hadn't thought about how her being here had affected his life.

The woman chuckled. "Schoolmates and then some, right, Mac?" She tilted her head so that her long, shiny brown locks rested on his shoulder.

"Ancient history, Lola." Mac stepped back and raised the hatch of his car.

"Well, I didn't mean to interrupt," the woman said, staring at him with bright, interested eyes. Jane knew that look, the way one female knows when another is flirting, even if the man is too dim to figure it out.

"Good seeing you again, Mac. Don't be a stranger."

Mac nodded and headed for the driver's door. "Take care, Lola."

Jane took her seat quietly and closed her eyes, stunned by her own rude behavior. "I'm really putting a damper on your social life."

Mac gunned his car out of Colorado Chuck's parking lot. Both were silent on the short drive home until he parked the car in his driveway.

Jane made a move to exit the car.

"Jane, listen."

She turned to him, her eyes bright with unshed tears. She couldn't name all the emotions churning around inside her gut, but she did know one thing. She didn't want Lola, or any other woman, hovering around Mac. And that made no sense at all. Jane had no right to him. He was free to see any woman he wanted, except her. He'd made that clear, yet when he'd showed up at the bookstore tonight, Jane's rational mind had shut down and she'd lost herself in foolhardy notions.

"Mac, don't try to convince me that my being here hasn't changed your life."

"Damn it, Jane. You're not stopping me from anything."

"You're just being sweet," she said softly.

Mac stormed out of the car, slamming the door. "I'm not *sweet*," he said, grinding out the words.

Jane stepped out of the car as well and together they walked up the steps to the front door. "Okay, so you're not that sweet. I never really thought so. Feel better now?" she said, smiling.

Mac paused, pursing his lips and blinking. "You never really thought so?"

She shook her head, so hard her hair whipped against her cheeks.

Mac ran a hand down his face in what she feared was utter frustration, but when she could finally see his mouth, the corners had lifted up and he laughed. "What am I going to do with you?"

She joined in the laughter, happy to have gotten him out of his bad mood. Then on impulse, she planted a quick kiss on his cheek. "Talk to me?"

Mac's eyebrows rose. "About?"

"About Lola, and how I'm not interfering in your life."

She sauntered past him when he unlocked the door, and stood waiting for his answer, arms folded.

Mac stared at her a moment, then his gaze dropped down to her chest, where she'd crossed her arms. Jane didn't flinch, though the heat of his perusal was enough to knock her off her feet.

Mac broke eye contact and moved to the window, his arms braced on the windowsill as he focused his gaze into the darkness of the night. "Lola and I are friends, Jane. Nothing more. We dated a while, after my divorce, but that's the end of it. We both moved on."

"She's not married."

Mac turned to her. "No. She'd drive any man insane, and you didn't hear that from me."

Jane chuckled, garnering satisfaction that Mac hadn't found the brunette irresistible. "Why?"

"Never mind. I've said enough."

"And what about other women, Mac? You're not dating anyone. You don't have a girlfriend. I find that hard to believe, since you're so…"

"So hard to deal with?" he finished for her. "Or maybe, stubborn? Too dedicated to my work? Name any of the above."

Jane softened her expression and took a seat on the sofa, looking up at him. "I was going to say so easy on the eye."

Mac sat down on the opposite end of the couch. He looked at her with a gleam in his eyes. "Now you're being sweet. But the truth is, sure, there are women who occasionally look me up. Sometimes I date, but it'll never amount to anything. I'm not looking for anything permanent. I've done the marriage thing. It isn't for me."

What a waste, Jane thought. Mac had too many great qualities to give up on sharing a life with someone.

"Too bad," she said aloud.

"I'm happy with my existence, Jane. Why do all the women in my life feel the need to push me into something I don't want? And," he said, leaning forward, pointing his index finger her way, "that goes for you, too. You're so sure you're wrecking my social life, but the truth is I don't have one. So no more talk about that. Don't worry, Jane."

"So, you really didn't want to spend time with Lola tonight?"

"I'm here with you, aren't I?"

Jane nearly snorted. "I guess I have my answer. Tell me, just where, exactly, did you go to charm school?"

"What?"

She cast him a slow smile and stood. "It's nothing, Mac. I think it's time for bed."

She walked over to him to say good-night, endeared to him more than she should be. Mac had been earnest with her. He'd shared part of his life. He'd tried to explain himself to her, the best he knew how. And now he stood before her, blocking her way to the hall leading to her room.

"Don't worry about anything but regaining your memory," he said, touching the tip of her nose.

The touch carried her over the edge. This time she kissed him fully on the mouth, surprising them both. Mac groaned, but he didn't back off. Instead, he wrapped both arms around her and held her loosely, allowing her to lead the way.

Jane knew she was in deep trouble the minute their lips met again. She'd longed for this, for his lips to warm hers and for the heat of their bodies to carry them away. "Definitely not sweet, Mac. But so much more." She parted her lips and their tongues met, the mating a sacred kind of homecoming.

Mac tightened his hold on her, drawing her up against

him so that she felt his heart beating, each pulse in sync with her own. "Sometimes you amaze me, Jane," he whispered into her mouth.

"I amaze myself, too," she whispered back.

Just as their lips met again, Lizzie barged into the room, stopping short the minute she spotted them. "Oh, sorry!"

Jane immediately backed away from Mac and stared at his sister, the red heat of embarrassment climbing up her throat.

Lizzie, on the other hand, was beamimg. "On second thought, I'm not sorry. It's about time!"

"Lizzie." Mac offered up a stern warning. "You and I need to have a little talk."

"Can't, big brother. I'm all packed. I'm leaving first thing in the morning for Raleigh."

"Okay, then, we'll talk on the way to the airport. What time?"

Lizzie smiled at Jane, her eyes bright with appreciation. "Oh, I already have a ride to the airport. Jane made the arrangements for me."

Mac looked at Jane with a quizzical expression. "You made arrangements for her? How?"

She smiled tentatively at Lizzie, ignoring his intense stare.

"Jane?" Mac moved to face her. "What did you do?"

"Nothing much, really," she said, trying to shrug it off.

Impatient with her evasion, he turned to his sister. "So, who's taking you to the airport?"

Chin up, Lizzie tossed out the one name that could make Mac crazy. "Deputy Lyle Brody."

* * *

Two nights later, Jane shelved the last of the children's books, tidied up the reading cove and met Jimmy at the cash register.

"All done," he said, his blond hair flipping onto his forehead when he glanced up. Jane liked Jimmy a lot and she was sure with his clean-shaven, earnest good looks, he would melt more than one young girl's heart. Yet he was always polite, a hard worker, and she knew that his grandfather adored him.

"So am I."

Both headed for the front door, Jane watching Jimmy lock it up good and tight before turning to her. "Are you sure you don't need a ride home?"

"I'm sure. Sheriff Riggs will be here shortly," Jane said, glancing up and down the darkened street, looking for Mac's black Trailblazer. Sometimes he picked her up in his patrol car, so she kept an eye out for that, too. She found it odd that he wasn't parked outside waiting for her. Mac never arrived late to pick her up. "You go on home, Jimmy. I'll be fine."

Jimmy frowned, shaking his head, but with a little more urging, Jane finally convinced him to leave. She stood outside Touched with Love, waiting. When Mac didn't appear for five full minutes, she began walking. She didn't mind. She had a lot to go over in her head, and the hot summer day had finally cooled to a warm breezy evening.

Mac had been furious with her the other night, and she'd walked in the chilling shadow of his cold shoulder for the past two days. He hadn't been happy with her interference in Lizzie's life. He'd been blunt, almost cruel. She'd never forget the look of contempt on his face once Lizzie had left the room that night.

"It's none of your concern, Jane," he'd said sternly. "You don't know all of it," he'd added. "You have no right butting into my business."

That last statement stung, and she'd tried defending herself valiantly, but Mac wouldn't hear anything she had to say. He'd simply shut down, refusing to discuss Lyle or Lizzie or why he felt so strongly about Lizzie getting involved with his deputy.

Jane had no choice but to back off, but the damage had been done. Mac barely tolerated her now, keeping a safe distance away even though she'd catch him at times peering at her from across the room. Still, the budding friendship they'd slowly developed had vanished.

Mac had never once made her feel like an intruder, but she had to believe that now he wanted her gone. Perhaps she should consider Dr. Quarles's invitation. Maybe it was time to leave Mac's home. There was no telling how long it would take to regain her memory.

She hadn't had any new revelations lately. She hadn't recalled anything else other than that she owned custom-made leather boots crafted in some small village in Italy. Nothing much had happened with the media blitz the sheriff's department had put out, either. Oh, there'd been one guy claiming her as his fiancée, but it turned out the man had been investigated as a single white male who had failed relationships with three online dating services. Jane couldn't help feeling sorry for him, but at the same time she'd been greatly relieved to find that she wasn't in any way tied to him.

There was only one man Jane wanted in her life and he was late picking her up. And just as she turned the corner on Elkwood Street, she heard the familiar rumble of a motor from behind.

Mac pulled up close to her, slowing the patrol car. He rolled down the window and Jane's ready smile disappeared. "Get in, Jane" was all he said, a deep frown marring his handsome face.

She raced around to the passenger side and slipped in. Realizing that something was wrong, she turned to him immediately. His face was bloodied and bruised, and he held one hand to his chest. Jane quaked with fear. "Mac, you're hurt."

The car moved forward and Mac nodded ever so slowly, the action causing him to wince even more. "Bad asses thought they could wreck Sully's place. Had to go in there and straighten them out."

Her mind jumbled, all she could think about was the extent of Mac's injuries. He still held that hand to his chest and hadn't let go. Blood oozed down his face where he'd been cut. "Where are you hurt?"

"Probably bruised a few ribs. Got a few cuts and scrapes. That's all."

"All?" Jane couldn't stand to see him in any pain. "You need to go to the hospital, Mac."

"No way, Jane. I'm fine."

"You don't look fine," she said, her voice rising. "You look like you've been run over by a truck."

"Gee, thanks. Appreciate the thought."

"I'm not kidding, Mac. Just how many were there, and what kind of place is Sully's, anyway?"

"About half a dozen. Bar and grill," he answered, his tone clipped. Jane feared he had broken, not bruised, ribs.

"Six of them and how many of you?"

"Two of us, until we got backup."

Jane's heart pounded. Up until tonight she hadn't thought much about Mac's profession, the dangers and pitfalls. Winchester was a small, quiet town. But seeing him in pain, barely able to drive, she felt the reality of Mac's job hit her with stark and unnerving force. Just like any other professional lawman, Mac put his life on the line each and every day. Jane couldn't shake that notion loose. It stayed with her, swamping her with fear. Then she noticed that his shirtsleeve was rolled up. "Looks like your arm is bandaged. What happened?" she asked.

"It's just a cut."

"A cut? Are you saying someone attacked you with a knife?"

He nodded. "Assault with a deadly weapon. It's been taken care of. The paramedic team patched me up."

Jane's gut tightened. Dear God. Mac could have been killed tonight. And that thought nearly destroyed her. Her feelings for Mac Riggs ran deeper than she'd believed. "Why didn't they take you to the hospital?"

Mac lifted one shoulder in a small shrug as he pulled into his driveway. And then it dawned on her. The paramedics would have taken Mac to the hospital if he had allowed them to. Instead, he'd shown up on Elkwood Street in his patrol car to pick her up. "I'm fine, Jane." He killed the engine and got out of the car.

Jane raced around the vehicle to meet him at the driver's side door. He stepped away from the SUV, hunching over a bit as he did so.

"Lean on me," she said firmly, bracing his body with hers.

He pursed his lips, deciding, then finally nodded once Jane had given him her most obstinate look. He wrapped his good arm around her shoulders and she braced his weight the best she could.

Together, they made their way slowly to the front door. Mac handed her the key and she opened the lock, then slanted her body sideways so they both would fit through the opening. Once inside, Jane led Mac to his bedroom.

She helped him sit down on his bed, and he took a minute, breathing deeply.

"Is your head spinning?" she asked.

He let out a wry chuckle. "You might say that. Of all the ways I've dreamed of getting you into my bedroom, this wasn't one of them."

Jane smiled, reveling in his earnest admission. "Lie down, Sheriff."

Mac obeyed, closing his eyes as he lowered his head and stretched out his long legs on the bed. Jane fussed with his pillow, propping it behind him.

She gave the pillow one last blow, then stood over Mac, gazing down at him. "You know, this isn't exactly how I'd hoped to get into your bedroom, either."

He opened one eye and peered at her, but she held her stance, refusing to let any embarrassment come through. The truth was the truth. "Now, stay put. Your forehead is bleeding again. I'll be right back."

She walked out of the room to the sound of Mac's groan. This time she knew it wasn't pain causing it, but her remark. At least Mac knew where she stood. There would be no second-guessing and no mistake. Jane wanted him, but tonight she'd realized something even more powerful. When she'd seen him bruised, battered and in so much pain, she knew she couldn't deny her feelings any longer. She knew that to lose him would be to lose herself all over again. She'd fallen for him.

Jane Doe was crazy in love with Sheriff Mac Riggs.

She took a minute to let her feelings sink in and accept what had been inevitable. She'd seen it coming, yet hadn't the power to deny or refuse the love that had begun building from the first moment she'd looked up into Mac's piercing dark eyes on that canyon road.

With a heavy sigh, Jane grabbed the first-aid kit out of the bathroom and gathered up the other supplies she needed, then headed back to Mac's room. She found him lying on the bed right where she'd left him, with eyes wide open, watching her.

She scooted next to him and dabbed at his head wound, the antiseptic oozing onto the cut above his eye. "Sorry, this must sting."

He grunted a denial.

"I think your ribs might be broken."

"Nah. I've broken ribs before when I played quarterback for the Wildcats. I know the difference. They're bruised, that's all."

Jane knew she had to get Mac more comfortable on his bed. "Can you get out of your clothes, or do you want me to do it?"

Mac cocked her a lopsided smile. "You do it."

Jane snorted. "This isn't funny, Mac. You scared me half out of my mind. It wasn't so thrilling seeing you bloody and bruised, slumped over the steering wheel. I just about had a heart attack."

"Sorry, Jane." He reached for her hand and she allowed him to hold it. He stroked his thumb gently across her palm, sending goose bumps all over her body. "Fact is, Winchester is a quiet town. We don't get a lot of excitement around here." He winced, his eyes shutting briefly, and she sensed the pain he was trying hard to conceal. "But June has been an unusual month. First with a beautiful amnesia victim landing on my doorstep and then tangling with a bunch of out-of-towners looking for trouble."

"Don't forget the joyriders abandoning cars in the lake."

"That, too. But for the most part, my job's pretty mundane. It's been a curious time in Winchester lately. Now, didn't I hear something about you undressing me?"

Jane twisted her mouth. "Taking unfair advantage, Sheriff?"

"Just need a little TLC, Jane." Then he lowered his voice, brought his lips to her outstretched palm and kissed her there. "From you."

Jane's heart stopped with that kiss, the moisture from

his lips seeping into her skin. Reluctantly, she pulled her hand free to reach for the buttons on his uniform shirt. Carefully, she unfastened each one, then gently slid the shirt off his shoulders. She held back her own wince when she saw up close the bruises on his chest and the bandage on his arm.

Jane dipped a washcloth into a bowl of water and cooled down his heated skin, her fingers sliding leisurely over his chest. On impulse, she bent down to plant a tiny kiss on one of the larger bruises. Mac lifted his good arm and stroked her head, weaving his fingers through her hair. Then he guided her head up and leaned forward, showing Jane what he wanted. Their lips met briefly, a sweet, healing kiss that made her heart flip and Mac smile. "You give great TLC."

Jane withdrew, stood up and headed for the end of the bed. She took a daunted look at his boots, then, with a steadying breath, pulled and twisted and finally yanked, until one boot came off, sock and all. "Not such good TLC here," she offered.

"I'm not complaining."

The other boot came off easier, and Jane felt a surge of satisfaction. She walked over to Mac, lying there bare-chested, looking vulnerable and sexy all at the same time.

"Can you manage your pants?" she asked, holding her breath.

Mac tried leaning forward, then bit back a howl of pain. He rested his head on his pillow. "Don't think so."

"Okay," Jane said, reaching for his belt. She unhooked it, then slid her hands down to his zipper, the evidence of his bulging manhood hard to miss. "Mac, I thought you were injured."

He didn't bother holding back a devilish smile. "Nothing hurts below the waist."

Jane stared down at him.

"Touch me there, and I can't be responsible for my actions."

Jane swallowed. "Is that an invitation or a warning?"

"Both," Mac said, the teasing glint in his eyes gone now. The heat of his gaze penetrated her, warming her all over. "It's crazy, you know. Denying what we both want."

Apparently, Mac had sifted though his own denials, to come up with the truth, too. "I know," she whispered, though she knew that she wouldn't deny Mac anything, not ever again.

Jane reached for his zipper.

Eight

Mac had been furious with her when she'd butted into Lizzie's business. He hadn't wanted anyone, especially Jane, to interfere in his relationship with Lizzie. Jane had just come to Winchester and she didn't know his history. She didn't know the heartache Mac had endured trying to salvage an unsalvageable marriage. She didn't know how Lyle Brody had interfered on his sister's behalf, causing even more strife between them.

But the minute he'd walked out of Sully's tonight, bloodied and bruised, the knife swipe having just missed his chest, cutting instead into the beefy part of his arm, all Mac could think about was Jane.

Getting to her.

Seeing her.

Wanting her.

He'd wasted too much time with her, too much of his life. That close call had him forgiving Jane everything. He'd forgotten all about his anger, and thought only about being with her.

And as she slowly slid his zipper down, the proof of his feelings were reflected in a powerful erection that only Jane could satisfy.

He watched her work his pants off without too much difficulty. She looked at him tentatively as she held his trousers to her chest protectively. "Wish I could undress *you*," he admitted softly.

Jane smiled, her lips parting in a subtle move. She dropped his pants, letting them fall at her feet. Without a second thought, she removed her tank top, the material catching on her breasts before being flipped over her head.

Mac sucked in oxygen. "Wow," he muttered, watching her necklace catch the moonlight where it nestled in the hollow between her breasts. She wore the jewelry he'd given her every day, and he'd felt a stirring of pride and possession.

She stood beside him now and leaned over. "You could unhook me."

Mac reached up behind her to unfasten her bra. He tugged slightly and the white cotton undergarment fell through his fingers. Her breasts toppled out, full and lush, and he groaned. "You're killing me, Jane."

"That's not what I had in mind to do to you, Mac." She bent down for a kiss, but he grabbed her around the waist, pulled her onto the bed and settled her on his thighs. She straddled him, her legs on either side of him. But he needed to feel her, skin to skin, so he guided her body down until her breasts rested on his chest.

His lips met hers urgently, sealing their fate with a long, hot, wet kiss that went on and on. He drove his tongue into her mouth, searching for and finding its mate. They sparred and teased and played feverishly, Mac stroking his hands through her soft blond hair, his fingers tugging and releasing the strands.

The feel of her breasts pressing into his chest, the soft subtle sounds she made, the unabashed passion she gave him were almost too much. Mac didn't think his erection could become any more potent.

Finally, she pulled away slightly, her breathing as labored as his. "I'm crushing your chest. It must hurt," she said.

Mac shook his head. "Only when you leave me."

Jane bit her lip, unsure.

"I mean it, sweetheart. You're not hurting me."

Jane settled back down, and Mac realized that nothing had felt better, or more right, in his whole life.

He kissed her deeply again, then lifted her easily at the waist, guiding her higher so that he could moisten the very tip of her nipple with his tongue.

"Oh, Mac," she moaned as he cupped her breast and continued to slide his tongue up and around and over the rosy tip until it peaked and pebbled.

Her next long, pleasured moan nearly brought him to the edge. "I need to be inside you, Jane," he managed to gasp, his voice hoarse with need.

He reached down to her jeans and fumbled with her zipper. Jane helped him, and he almost lost it again when she shimmied out of her pants. She helped get his boxers off, then did a little wiggle to get out of her own panties.

"Reach over to my nightstand, sweetheart. We need protection."

Mac prayed he still had a condom or two in there. It'd been a while.

When Jane carefully slid across him, coming up with one, Mac silently sighed with relief and quickly managed to secure the condom in place.

He held her waist and guided her body, positioning her over him and lowering her. He slipped his full erection inside her, joining them together with one slow, deliberate thrust.

As she took him in, she closed her eyes, parted her moist lips and tossed her head back as if savoring the moment. Mac had never seen anything quite so beautiful in his whole life. Deep, heady sensations washed over him as he watched this sexy, mysterious woman slowly move on him, her body's natural instincts taking hold as she raised and lowered with each of his thrusts.

In sync, in rhythm, they moved together, Jane huffing out little throaty breaths and Mac moving more forcefully now as their momentum escalated, higher and higher.

He reached up to caress her breasts, rubbing his thumbs over her peaked tips until she ground out his name. The intense look on her face brought him a new brand of pleasure as he watched her ride the waves of their passion. Up and down, faster, harder. Mac took hold of Jane's hands, interlacing their fingers, connecting them in every way possible.

He felt her shudder. Her muttered moans and pleas as she breathed out his name gave him the ultimate satisfaction. "Oh, Mac."

He plunged deeper, thrusting one final time as she came down hard, and then, in tandem, they both shuddered violently with completion.

Mac lay breathless, Jane atop him.

They stared into each other's eyes.

Moments ticked by and yet neither spoke.

Jane appeared a little stunned.

Mac felt the same way.

Finally, he lifted his lips in a crooked, cocky smile.

Jane smiled back.

Then he kissed her deeply. "That was worth the wait."

Jane slid her body sideways to curl up beside him, her arms wrapped around his neck. "Mmm. I don't think I've ever…um."

Mac lifted his head to stare down at her. "Ever?"

She cast him a shy smile. "Not that. I mean, I don't think it's ever been so good."

He inhaled deeply. "You don't know that, for sure."

"Oh, I think I do, Mac."

He trusted her on that one. Of course, it did his ego good to do so, and he believed a woman would simply *know* those things. But there was so much to Jane that neither of them knew about. There was so much he wanted to know and so much he feared knowing.

He reminded himself that her memory could return

at any moment, but it was too late for guarding against his heart. He couldn't think rationally when it came to Jane. Not anymore. Not after tonight.

For once in his life, Mac took a chance that fate might work in his favor. He couldn't think past that. He didn't want to. This time around, he would take a gamble.

Jane was worth the risk.

Bacon sizzled in the pan, eggs boiled and Jane stared out the kitchen window, still in awe, her body humming from making love to Mac last night. He'd been breathing strongly and steadily when she'd left him minutes ago to allow him the rest he needed. He'd been injured last night, and Jane couldn't contain the fear she'd felt seeing him bruised like that. She couldn't contain her relief, knowing that his injuries weren't life threatening. But mostly Jane couldn't contain the love swelling up inside her. Deep, fresh emotions sang in her veins, and her heart was awash with guarded joy. She wanted to feel every sensation, let it seep in and take hold, but a part of her held back. A part of her worried about Mac's reaction.

He had been reserved—resigned, really, to not getting emotionally involved with her. He'd been the responsible one, the one who faced facts. Jane didn't know her past, but that didn't mean she didn't have one.

She prayed that Mac wouldn't wake up this morning and tell her that they'd made a mistake last night. She couldn't bear the blow to her heart if that happened.

Just as that thought settled in her gut, Mac stepped up behind her, wrapping his arms around her waist and dragging her body up against his. She leaned back against him, resting her head just under his throat.

"Morning," he said, nibbling her earlobe, his lips warm and inviting.

"Oh, Mac," she said quietly, relishing the feel of his arms around her once again. "It is a good morning, isn't it?"

"The best," he said softly, running his hands up and down her rib cage in a soft, sensual caress.

The frying pan crackled as the scent of bacon permeated the air, reminding her of the breakfast she'd wanted to present to Mac this morning.

She turned around in his arms to look at his face. Dark patches of bluish-purple appeared harsher in the daylight, more pronounced, but his eyes held hers with warmth and feeling. She reached up to gently outline a bruise just above his temple. "How are you this morning?"

"Pretty darn good, sweetheart."

"Really? I thought after you got hurt last night you'd wake up sore. How's your chest? Can I do anything to—"

He bent his head and kissed her soundly, pretty much cutting off her words. She had trouble formulating any coherent thoughts as well, falling into the kiss with total abandon. Mac was a take-charge kind of guy, and Jane decided she liked that about him, especially now as his mouth claimed hers and his hands took charge, roaming over her backside, stirring up wildly wicked thoughts.

"That'll do just fine," he said, ending the kiss and

taking a step back. He sighed and scrubbed his jaw. "I missed you in bed this morning."

"I wanted to make you breakfast. You need your nourishment, Mac. Especially after last night."

He cocked her a lopsided smile. "Seems to me I held up pretty well. You're the one who didn't want a second—"

"Mac!" Jane's jaw dropped. She couldn't believe he would be so open and earnest about their lovemaking. Jane hadn't wanted to exhaust him after he'd been involved in an altercation that left his ribs bruised and his body battered. It had been hard refusing him, and Lord knew she wanted him again, but she'd been worried about his physical condition. "I was speaking about the fact that you'd been in a fight last night."

Mac laughed and spun around to turn the knob on the stove. "Appreciate the thought, but I'll have to take a rain check on breakfast. I'm late getting to the station. I need to make out my report."

Jane hid her disappointment. She'd hoped it wouldn't be business as usual today. "Okay."

"Are you…okay?" he asked. "About what happened last night?"

She wouldn't pretend; she knew he was referring to the night they'd spent in bed together. "It was wonderful, Mac."

"Yeah," he said, and then he sighed again. "Are you going to the bookstore today?"

She nodded. "I had planned on it."

"Could you take the afternoon off?"

"Sure. Do you need me to do something? Is it regarding my case?"

He shook his head. "No, nothing like that. I'm going in to fill out my report, then I'm taking some time off. There's something…someplace I want to show you. Will you come with me?"

Does the sun shine? Is Paris a city? "I'd love to."

"Great, I'll pick you up at the bookstore later on. Oh, and wear comfortable clothes, nothing fancy, and don't wear those boots. They'd get ruined where we're going."

"Is this all yours?" Jane asked, her gaze roaming across the land surrounding a beautiful adobe ranch house. Mac had driven twenty miles out of town, to the verdant side of a mesa. Pike's Peak could be seen in the distance, and he had pointed out the amazing Kissing Camels rock formation.

"About twenty acres of it is mine," he said, and she couldn't miss the obvious pride in his voice. "This place was a wreck when I bought it. The house was in shambles and the property was in foreclosure."

"How long have you had it?" she asked, still pretty much stunned at this new facet of Mac's life. He was a private man, with private thoughts, and the fact that he wanted to share this with her was nothing short of spectacular.

"About eight years. I've been working on the house in my spare time."

Eight years? About the length of time Mac had been

divorced. Jane wondered if he'd needed a place, something to rebuild, something to make his own, after his marriage failed. Perhaps working on the house, fixing it up had been a sort of therapy for him.

"It's lovely."

He chuckled and guided her forward. "Wait until you see it up close before you say that."

Mac showed her in, and the massive ranch house instantly became a cozy refuge once she stepped foot inside. "I've got more work to do, but—"

"No buts, Mac," Jane said, taking a leisurely walk around, making note of a stone fireplace, wood beam ceilings, an inviting sitting area, wide bay windows that brought the outside prairie land inside. "This is unbelievable."

She turned to face him. He let out a deep breath and smiled. "I'm glad you like it."

"What's not to like?"

"Some people would think it too…rustic, too remote. It's just a rural home."

"It's more than that. I love it. When do you have time to come up here?"

"Weekends when I'm not working. Vacations. It's not so far that I can't stop by in the evenings, either. Sometimes Duke and Daisy Mae get lonely."

Jane raised her brows in question.

"My horses. Well, Duke is mine. I bought Daisy Mae for Lizzie. She comes up and rides with me once in awhile. I hired the neighbor's daughter, Angie, to feed and ride them when I can't get up here. She's real good with the horses. I was hoping you'd like to ride today. Do you know how?"

Jane thought for a moment, unsure. "I don't think so. But I'm willing to learn."

Mac smiled.

Overwhelmed with emotion, she walked over to him. "I'm glad you brought me here. It's a lovely home and I want the whole nickel tour." Then she put her arms around his neck, tugging him down to her level. When he expected her kiss, Jane surprised him instead by whispering quietly near his mouth, "A tour that ends in your bedroom, Mac. Do you think the horses will mind waiting?"

Mac pulled her closer, her body meshing fully against his hard, tight length. He took her lips in a long, sweeping kiss that left her completely breathless. "We'll give them extra carrots."

This time Mac did undress her, and he took his own sweet time. He peeled one article off after another, with calculated moves that swamped her body with slow, simmering heat. He touched her, caressed her and kissed her with such unhurried deliberation that she wanted to scream out.

"Be patient with me," he said, standing by his massive cedar-and-oak four-poster bed. "I want to know all of you."

Jane stood before him, watching afternoon light cast him in sun and shadows, defining his strong jawline and dark intense eyes. And when she was fully unclothed, she reached for him, to begin unbuttoning his shirt.

"No, not yet," he said, taking her shoulders and spinning her around. He brought her up against him, her derriere to his groin, her back to his chest. With a hand, he pushed her hair to one side and nibbled on her neck, planting light kisses there while the other hand held her hip, keeping her body firmly in place.

"Relax, Jane," he whispered in a husky tone.

Heart racing, Jane knew that was impossible to do. Her soft skin pressed against his rough jeans and she felt the heat of his hard, tight shaft. She took a deep breath and his heady musky scent enveloped her. "Mac," she muttered, but no other words formed. None were necessary.

His hands came up to stroke her breasts, the twin round globes aching for his touch. He stroked her gently, almost reverently, and whispered on a breath, "You're perfect, sweetheart."

Jane's legs nearly buckled, her body weakening at his touch. She rested against him, arching up, and Mac groaned, tightening his hold on her, rubbing her skin more fervently now.

He roamed over her body, splaying his hands, sizing her up, his fingers exploring every inch of her. With one palm on her belly, he let the other slide lower, and Jane felt a burning warmth between her thighs. Raw heat coursed through her, and when Mac finally found her core, cupping her, she moaned with relief, letting out a little gasp.

Mac kissed her neck again, moistening her skin with his tongue, while he continued to stroke her. Her body instinctively moved, and they swayed together as he continued his ministrations. His fingers parted her skin, and he found her center. Electric sparks flew, her body picking up the rhythm of his strokes. Her release building, Jane gave in, letting herself go. She moved without thought, without shame. Mac urged her from behind with sweet, sexy words that she felt more than heard.

Her climax exploded, shattering her and making every sensation become more vivid, more intense. Her pleasure heightened, but the love she felt for Mac wedged its way even deeper into her heart.

She collapsed against him, letting him hold her as she slowly recovered.

Outside, she heard the trees rustling and birds chirping, but inside, she heard only the beating of her heart.

Mac waited patiently, holding her without saying a word, as if he knew she needed this time. And when she was ready, she turned to face him.

His eyes sharpened on her, the brown nearly black and his expression unguarded, open. "I need you inside me now," she said, whispering the same words he had said to her last night.

Mac smiled as he dug into his pocket, then removed a handful of condoms. He tossed them onto the night-stand. Jane took one glance and grinned.

She lay down on the bed and waited. Mac undressed in front of her, his body gleaming and more than ready. He came down beside her.

"I want to know all of you," she said boldly, reaching for him.

Mac groaned as she took him in her hand. "I've always liked a woman with a thirst for knowledge."

"Really?" Jane's own voice was husky now. Unmercifully, she stroked the silky length of him. "Then relax and enjoy the ride, Mac. 'Cause there's a lot I want to learn."

Nine

Jane stroked Daisy Mae's mane, the coarse hair sliding beneath her palms. "Hi there, Daisy Mae. You're a pretty one, aren't you?"

The mare nuzzled her throat in response, seemingly happy to be out of the stable and in the fresh late-afternoon air.

"Careful," Mac said, "she's good-natured, but she doesn't know you yet."

Jane smiled. "I think we're going to be friends."

Mac stared at her for a moment, then nodded. "She's a chestnut quarter horse. Workhorses back in the Old West, but now she's got it soft."

Jane glanced at the ink-black horse that stood alongside Mac, nudging him occasionally for attention. "What about Duke?"

"Duke's a gelding quarter and a great guy." Mac stroked the horse's snout with tender care, much like he'd made love to Jane, just an hour ago. For all his gruff ways, Jane couldn't miss the gentle side to Sheriff Mac Riggs. He was hard as steel when he had to be, but Jane had seen his tender side, and both facets of the man fascinated her.

"Want to give it a try?" Mac said, gesturing toward the two saddles in a paddock to her right.

"Sure. As long as you take it slow."

He nodded and cast her one of his killer smiles. "I can do that."

Heat crawled up her neck. Jane remembered how well Mac could take it slow. So much so that her breath hitched as she recalled how controlled, how incredibly restrained Mac could be, just to ensure her own pleasure. "Okay, then."

Mac saddled both horses, giving her quick directions. "Mount from the left, hold the reins loose, but with enough tension to let Daisy know you're in control." He ran his hand along Jane's upper thigh, the simple touch enough to make her heart race. "Use this part of your body to lean in and let her know which way you want to turn. Horses understand body language. Don't solely rely on the reins."

Jane nodded, peering up into his dark eyes. "Okay, I think I've got it."

Mac helped her mount, handed her the reins and looked up at her. "Don't let Daisy know you're worried.

Ride with confidence. I've got your back, Jane. I won't let anything happen to you."

Jane let out the breath she'd been holding. For all she knew, this was the first time she'd ever been atop a horse. "I trust you, Mac."

His brows rose and something powerful flashed in his eyes. "Okay, here we go."

Mac mounted Duke, and Jane was amazed at how much taller he sat on his horse. She pictured him as a sheriff in the Old West, ready to lead a posse out on the range to capture a villain. Silently she laughed at the thought, but her amusement caught his eye.

"What?"

She shook her head. "Nothing. It's just that you look like you belong here, Mac. This place suits you."

He leaned over and kissed her quickly, the familiar warmth of his lips sending her heart racing again. "Let's go."

Mac led the way, and Daisy seemed to follow Duke without any help from Jane. Before long, Jane forgot that she sat upon a horse, instead enjoying the scenery and Mac's comments about the land and history of the area. They rode the perimeter of his property as the sun began its descent behind the mountain range.

Mac had them back at the house before dusk, Jane insisting on helping him bed down the horses for the night. Daisy Mae didn't seem to mind Jane's unsure hands as she used the leather-handled body brush, making sure she cleaned the brush with the curry comb. She worked as hard as Mac, giving Daisy a good brushing as Mac explained it helped to keep her skin clean and open up her pores. Then, with great care, she sponged Daisy's eyes and nostrils, cleaning them and washing her down.

"I'm impressed," Mac said as they entered the house.

"You are?"

He nodded. "Lizzie hates the clean-up part. Especially using the water brush on Daisy's tail."

Jane laughed. "I can see why. It's dangerous back there."

Mac chuckled, too, swinging his arms around her. He locked his hands behind her back, trapping her against him. "You're grimy, Jane. I think you need a shower."

"You're a mess, too, Mac." She lifted her nose in the air. "And is that horse dung I smell on you?"

"There's only one shower," he said, eyes twinkling. "That's all we need."

Their clothes were off by the time they reached the bathroom. Mac entered first, adjusting the temperature, getting the water just right. "It's safe to come in."

Jane stepped inside, realizing that Mac's big muscular body took up most of the space. "I'd hardly call this safe." She gulped, staring at him as water rained down on her.

Mac didn't respond. Instead, he took the bar of soap and began lathering her all over. His slick hands soaped her up and down, his palms both smooth and a little rough on her skin. Raw need rippled through her body as Mac touched every part of her, his hands moving on her possessively.

She went through periods of holding her breath, then letting it out in a pleasured sigh. Mac massaged her backside thoroughly, the scented soap slipping and sliding. Then he turned her around and worked her upper body, his hands skimming her breasts, the quick brief touches enough to make her cry out. He moved lower, soaping her belly, and lower yet, his hands spreading her legs, to clean her inner thighs. Every now and then he'd kiss her, sometimes on her lips and sometimes on the very part of her he was washing.

Hot water rained down, creating steam enough to fog the glass panes. Jane was sure that they'd be encased in their own cloud of passion, regardless. And when Mac had finished, he handed her the soap, claiming it was her turn.

Jane took hold of the soap and worked up lather on Mac's formidable chest, her hands spreading the tiny bubbles across it until he was richly coated. She slid her hands up and over, curling her fingers in the chest hairs, grazing his flat nipples until they peaked.

Neither could ignore Mac's full erection, which stood like a barricade against Jane's body, but she continued on, soaping him up, giving as good as she'd gotten. She lathered his strong thighs and bent to do his calves, eliciting a deep groan from Mac when she went higher to work her hands over that area of his body that had grown hard and tight.

But she wasn't quite through with Mac yet. She spun him around and massaged his broad shoulders, working down his back with the soap. Its citrus scent permeated the room as she continued on, moving lower, to caress the slope of his buttocks, and causing her a deep intake of breath. But before she could finish, Mac spun around abruptly, shaking his head. "Can't take much more, sweetheart."

Jane braved a glance downward and nodded, the sheer, massive power of him overwhelming. He bent his head, taking urgent claim to her lips, his tongue probing. The hungry kiss led to more caresses, more urgency, until Mac maneuvered Jane against the tiled wall of the shower. Out of the steady stream of spray now, he lifted her up and impaled her with his shaft, entering her in one long, full thrust.

"Oh, Mac," she cried, holding his shoulders and wrapping her legs around him.

"That's it, baby," he rasped, his hands behind her urging her on, and together they rode the wave of their passion.

Eyes closed and heart racing, Jane reeled with the heady sensations of slick bodies, heat and steam. She met each of Mac's thrusts, oblivious to all else, until one niggling, unwelcome thought struck. She stopped and opened her eyes. "Mac, wait."

He halted, his eyes dark with desire, but wide with curiosity. "What's wrong?"

"We have no protection," she said, her breaths labored.

Mac froze for a moment, deep in thought, then he shrugged. "Doesn't matter," he said, and the implication was clear. He wasn't speaking of health issues here, but the thought of conceiving a child. And Mac didn't seem to think it a problem. His quick admission told Jane in so many words that what they had went beyond a summertime fling. Her heart soared with the notion, and she tossed her reservations away. No matter what her other life might have to offer, Mac had to be in her life from now on, she knew.

"It doesn't?" she asked, only for clarification.

Mac shook his head. "Not to me," he said. "I want you to know that. But you're right. You can't afford to get caught up in something that might be bigger than both of us. You have another life somewhere out there, Jane. And it's my job to protect you."

Jane tugged him closer and brought her mouth to his in a long hot kiss. "Thank you, Mac."

He lifted her in his arms and brought her to the bedroom, protecting her from everything but the one thing that he couldn't control—her unquestionable love for him. They joined bodies once again, finishing what they had started, but their hot, urgent mood had suddenly changed to reverent caresses and sweet indulgence.

Mac woke in the early morning with Jane in his arms. He lay curled around her body, the fit and feel of her something he would never forget. Her freshly showered scent filled his nostrils as sunlight poured into his bedroom, casting golden light on her honey-blond hair. He tightened his hold on her, bringing his body even closer. They'd spent the night here, at the ranch, and Mac held close to his heart the memories of sleeping with her last night and waking to the soft sounds of her breathing. Aside from Lizzie, he hadn't brought another female here, to his refuge, his home away from home.

He smiled, thinking of Jane atop the horse, hanging on for dear life, and then later, her attempt to groom Daisy Mae. She'd been happy to learn, eager to participate. Mac hadn't met too many women like Jane Doe, the mystery lady with the unknown past.

He sighed deeply, the sound resonating inside the room. Jane turned in his arms and opened her pretty, lavender-blue eyes. "Hi."

"Morning," he said, kissing the dimples at the corners of her mouth. "It's a workday, sweetheart. I need to get going."

"Mmm."

"I'll see what I can find for breakfast. Must have some cereal and dry milk in the pantry."

"I'm not hungry, Mac."

"No, neither am I." He flopped onto his back, staring up at the ceiling. He let out another long sigh, one he couldn't contain. He had something to tell Jane, something that he should have told her yesterday.

"What's wrong?" she asked, her hand gently caressing his wounded arm. He turned to look into her eyes, finding concern there. "Did we overdo it yesterday? Is it your chest?"

She slipped her hand onto his torso, her fingers splaying across his ribs with tenderness.

He covered her hand with his and laced their fingers. "No. I'm feeling better, just bruised."

"Then what's up?" she asked, again with concern.

"When I went into the station yesterday to file my report, we had some news about your case. Seems the investigation has turned up eight potential shoemakers that design custom boots like yours. It'll take a few days to track down a list of their clients. The boots are high-end, as you know, ranging in price from two to three thousand dollars a pair."

Jane sat up on the bed and leaned forward, clutching the sheet to her bare chest. She looked so beautiful sitting there with hope filling her eyes that Mac couldn't pry his gaze away. Yet he ached for her in ways he never had before in his life. The lawman in him knew it was his duty to find out who she was and to return her to the life she'd once led, the one she'd had before he'd found her up on Deerlick Canyon. But Mac cursed the news, as well. He'd come to dread the day when Jane Doe found out her identity.

"Are you saying I might find out soon who I am? That one of the names on the list might be mine?"

Mac nodded, gauging Jane's reaction. She smiled then and lay her head down on her pillow slowly, her eyes bright with anticipation. "I wonder what my real name is. Where I live. There are so many things I've wondered about."

She reached for his hand and squeezed it. "Just think, Mac. In a few days I'll know who I am."

"Maybe. I don't want to get your hopes up. Not yet. Not until we have something more concrete. That's why I held off telling you. But now…well, I figured that you and I have to face facts."

Jane wrestled the sheets off and sat up on her knees, naked to the world and beautiful to him. "What facts?"

Mac remained silent. He was torn with wanting what was right for Jane and the nagging pain in his gut telling him that she'd be gone before long.

She stared into his eyes and he couldn't hide the indecision he felt, or the pain.

Jane immediately responded. "It won't change anything between us, Mac. It can't."

He tossed back the covers and got out of bed. "*Everything* is going to change, Jane. We can't pretend it won't." He picked up his clothes and began dressing.

"I wasn't pretending…about anything," she said honestly, before getting up and grabbing her own clothes.

Mac waited for her to slip on her pants and blouse. "I wasn't, either. Let's just wait and see what happens." He wrapped his arms around her to reassure her, but he had doubts. He'd been a fool to get involved with Jane in the first place. Hell, he'd tried not to. Tried to ignore every sweet aspect of her personality, the tempting allure of her sexy body and those big lavender eyes. But from day one, he'd been a goner, and now they'd both pay the price. The last thing he wanted to do was hurt her.

Jane rested her head on his chest. He brought her closer, their bodies touching intimately, with a familiarity Mac had known only one other time in his life, with his wife. But nothing compared to how Jane felt in his arms, the rightness of it. Desire surged again, but he held back, needing to hold her more than anything else.

"I never thought that learning my identity might hurt me."

"It won't, Jane. I promise it won't. You'll be glad when you find out about yourself."

She lifted her chin and he felt her eyes on him. "Will I?"

He nodded. "Yeah, you will."

"And what about you?"

"Me?" he asked, looking away, ignoring her penetrating gaze. He didn't want her to see his face when he told the biggest lie of his life. "I'll be glad, too, Jane. It's what we've been working for all this time. Now, we both have work to do today. Are you ready?"

Jane glanced around the ranch house with sadness in her eyes. "Yes, I'm ready. Let's go home."

The words stuck in Mac's head all the back to Winchester. He hadn't planned it, didn't know how or when it had happened, but he'd come to think of Jane as "home."

"What do you mean, you're moving out?" Mac interrogated Lizzie from across the parlor.

"Exactly what I said, Mac. I found a place and I'm moving out. It's time, big brother. Doesn't mean that I don't love you, or I don't appreciate you taking care of me all those years when I was a kid. But I'm not a kid anymore."

Jane watched the scene unfold from the doorway of the parlor, frozen to the spot. She'd known things would change between her and Mac when Lizzie arrived home this morning, but she couldn't have guessed this turn of events. Jane didn't want to interfere, felt it wasn't her place to listen in on this conversation, but Lizzie had asked her to be there, to act as a buffer when she told Mac the news. Jane couldn't refuse Lizzie's request. Both siblings had done so much for her. And she wanted to help Lizzie. She wanted to see her happy.

"Hell, I know you're not a kid. That's not what this is all about."

"It's about me gaining some independence. It's about giving you the space you need, Mac."

He gestured widely, his arms outstretched. "It's a big enough house. I have all the space I need."

"Then maybe I don't have all the space I need," she said quietly, looking at Jane. Jane nodded, giving her encouragement. Mac was formidable, a man you wouldn't want to cross, but Lizzie had rights, too, and Jane wouldn't refuse her support. "I found a place just a few miles from here, Mac. It's great, really. And I have plans for fixing it up."

Mac stared at her, then at Jane. He paced the floor, his face a study in fury. He shook his head over and over, breathing deeply.

Jane hated to see this confrontation. These past few days with Mac had been glorious. After they'd returned home from his ranch house, they'd gotten into a domestic routine like any other happy couple. Mac would go off to work and Jane would spend time volunteering at the bookstore. She'd come home and fix dinner, then they'd spend quiet time sitting together outside, talking about mundane things until they fell into bed. Nothing was mundane about their lovemaking, though. It was hot and passionate one time, then sweet and lazy the next.

The only bleak spot marring their days had been with the news that Jane's identity was still a mystery. The investigators, including Mac himself, had located every woman who'd had boots made by the eight shoe-makers on the list. Every one had checked out. Every single woman had been accounted for. Mac had come home that night with a dozen red roses, gently breaking the news to her. Jane had been sorely disap-pointed, her hopes dashed, but Mac had been so sweet and tender, holding her and making love to her throughout the night, that Jane had woken with a newfound feeling of hope. And it had little to do with learning her identity.

"Damn it!" Mac's curse brought her back. He threw his arms up, his voice filled with disgust. "Maybe Jane can talk some sense into you."

Jane walked over to him, put her hands on his arms and said gently, "Maybe you should *talk* to Lizzie, Mac. All you've been doing since she told you her plans is shout. Sit down and listen to her." Jane turned to Lizzie. "Both of you, listen to each other."

Mac opened his mouth to comment, but a knock at the door stopped him. He walked over and yanked the door open.

Deputy Lyle Brody stood on the threshold.

"Morning, Sheriff."

Mac grunted, his face grim. "Brody. What's up? Hell, it's Sunday. Is there a problem at the station?"

Standing tall, Lyle peered into the house, meeting Lizzie's eyes. He smiled, and Mac turned his head in his sister's direction to find Lizzie smiling back. Jane walked up to stand beside her. "Actually, boss, I came here to see Lizzie."

"This isn't a good—"

Lizzie rushed up and slipped out the door to stand right next to the deputy. "Hi, Lyle."

"Lizzie," Lyle said, "it's good to see you. Do you have time to take a walk with me?"

Lizzie turned her back on Mac and answered, "I'd love to."

Mac turned to Jane, his face wrought with emotion. He slammed the door after the two had taken off down the street. "What the hell's happening around here?"

Jane took his hand and led him over to the couch. "Sit."

He glared at her with defiance, but Jane knew him better than that. She knew his gruff facade was only window dressing, covering up a more vulnerable man underneath. That guarded vulnerability was one of the reasons she loved him so much. She reached up to kiss his lips, and gave a little shove. "Sit down."

The shove wouldn't have budged him if he hadn't wanted to comply. He sat down.

She planted herself atop his lap and wrapped her arms around him. "Things are changing, Mac. And it's okay."

"It's not okay."

"Lizzie doesn't want to hurt you. Don't make it

harder on her than it has to be. She adores you, Mac. But it's time to let her go."

"Don't give me the if-you-love-her-you'll-let-her-go speech, Jane."

Jane's chuckle broke the tension and she grinned. "You know me so well, Mac."

He didn't budge, his expression still grim. "What's she doing with him, anyway?"

"Lyle? She likes him. A lot. And apparently the feeling is mutual. She only wants your blessing. And in this day and age, I'd say that was something special."

Mac sighed heavily, closing his eyes. "He's not right for Lizzie."

"Mac, listen to me. I think I've figured out why you're so opposed to Lizzie seeing Lyle."

Mac tipped his chin up to listen, but with narrowed eyes. Jane knew she had to tread carefully. Mac was a prideful man who didn't like anyone analyzing his motives. "I'm listening."

"All your life you've been in control of things. You took care of Lizzie when she was younger, being both brother and father to her. You worked hard at your job, and built a wonderful career as a sheriff who is highly respected. You're handsome and strong and perfect in almost every way."

"I don't think of myself like that, Jane."

"I do."

His lips broke into a reluctant smile, but a smile nonetheless. "Yeah?"

She nodded. "Yeah."

"Are you trying to get me into bed, honey? Because I'm pretty much a sure thing."

Jane let out an unexpected chuckle. "I'm glad, but let's get back to the real subject here. I think that having Lyle around the station house is one thing, but you don't want to see him anywhere else. You don't want Lizzie to have a relationship with him, because every time you see him, it's a reminder of the one failure in your life, Mac. I'm not saying your divorce was your fault. I don't think it was, but Lyle Brody reminds you of something you couldn't fix. Something that you couldn't control. You don't have anything against Lyle personally. In fact, I think you like him. It's what he represents that bothers you."

Mac sat there quietly, absorbing her little speech, staring off into space.

"Am I close?" she asked.

He lifted her off of him, gently setting her down on the sofa, then stood up to face her. With hands on hips, he stared into her eyes, his expression pensive. "I don't know, Jane. I'll give it some thought."

Jane stood to face him, and her encouraging smile was enough for Mac at the moment. He couldn't remember a time when he'd been happier. She wrapped her arms around his neck, her expression so open and honest. "I meant all those things I said about you, Mac. You're a special man."

Mac had to face facts. He was crazy about Jane. *She* was the special one, the woman who had filled his life and brought him a kind of joy he'd never known before.

It was time he owned up to his emotions. It was time to admit to Jane what was in his heart. "Jane, I'm—"

A hard knocking at the door interrupted Mac's confession. With a deep sigh, he glanced at the front door. "Lizzie must have gotten locked out," he said, shuffling aside his annoyance. His sister had lousy timing, but he wasn't angry with her. Not anymore. Thanks to Jane, he decided to cut his sister some slack. "Maybe it wouldn't be such a bad thing to have her move out," he said, striding to the door. "At least this place would quiet down some."

"I'll be in kitchen making coffee," Jane said, grinning, and Mac figured she wanted to give him a chance to speak with his sister alone.

Mac opened the door. To his surprise, it wasn't Lizzie standing on the doorstep, but an impeccably dressed man with jet-black hair, looking him directly in the eye. "Sheriff Riggs?"

Mac nodded, a sense of dread he couldn't explain invading his chest.

"I'm here for Bridget Elliott."

Ten

Mac swallowed hard. He sized the man up in one quick moment and his instincts told him this was the real deal. The air of confidence about him, the way he looked Mac squarely in the eyes and his well-groomed appearance told the lawman that the mystery surrounding Jane Doe would soon be over.

In a smooth move, the stranger produced a wallet-size picture. His heart in his stomach, Mac took a quick look, seeing Jane smiling at the camera, with this man's arms around her. "You do recognize the woman in the photo? Is this the woman who's been living here?" he asked, and Mac came out of his stupor to realize that he should be the one asking questions.

"Before I answer that, let me ask how you arrived on my doorstep and who are you?"

The man shot him a no-nonsense look. "I've been searching for Bridget for ten days, Sheriff. I have contacts that led my search here."

Mac didn't miss the note of softness in the man's tone when he spoke Bridget's name.

Bridget?

Was Jane's name really Bridget Elliott?

"What kind of contacts? Who are you?"

"My contacts aren't any of your concern. All that matters is finding Bridget."

"I still don't know who you are," Mac said firmly.

"My name is Bryan. I'm Bridget's—"

"Mac, coffee's ready," Jane called out, and Mac gauged the man's reaction at hearing her voice. His eyes widened and he tried to peer into the house. "That's her voice," he said decisively. "May I?" He took a step forward to enter.

Mac wanted to block the doorway. He wanted to send this man packing. He didn't know a thing about him, except he *did* know. The truth. This man had come to take Jane home.

A soul-searing pain settled in Mac's gut. Everything inside him ached with the knowledge that Jane was lost to him now. This man named Bryan had come to claim her. A quick glance at his left hand said he wasn't married to her. But that didn't mean that they weren't deeply involved. Maybe engaged? All of Mac's initial fears and apprehensions had come full circle now. And another emotion he hated to admit tore at him. Jealousy. So deep, so raw, that it shook him to the core.

He forced himself to step away and allow the man entrance. Both men stood just inside the house.

"The coffee's hot, Mac," Jane said, coming out of the kitchen holding a steaming mug. She shot him a look, then her gaze flew to the man who called himself Bryan. "Oh hi, Bryan. What are doing…"

Jane stopped, the mug in her hand, shaking. She blinked, and Mac noted the revelations, her past instantly becoming her present, all reflected in her deep lavender eyes. She took a moment, as if she'd been hit with the fast-forward button to her life. There was no doubt that her memory had returned. He saw it all in her expressive face.

Slowly, she set the mug down, then smiled at Bryan with such warmth that Mac felt as though an elephant had trampled his body. "Bryan!"

She raced into his outstretched arms and he swung her around, lifting her off the ground, joy evident on both of their faces. "Oh my God," she said, "Oh, my God. You're here, you're really here."

Bryan set her down. "I'm here, honey. I've been searching for you. You gave us all a big scare."

"I had amnesia, Bryan. But everything came back to me. Just now. Seeing you. I can't believe it. Everything's back."

"That's great, honey," Bryan said, his gaze roaming over her, as if making sure she was all right. That proprietary look struck Mac like a sharp knife to the gut.

Mac had been the one seeing to Jane's welfare all this time. He'd reserved that right for himself.

"I'm glad I found you," Bryan continued. "What the hell happened to you?"

"I remember now," she began after a brief pause. "I flew to Colorado nearly two weeks ago, after Cullen's wedding. My rental car broke down, so I started walking up the canyon road. I fell and hit my head. That must have been when I lost my memory. Mac found me. He and his sister, Lizzie, took me in." She glanced at Mac, her face beaming. "Oh, sorry. Here I am, going on, and I haven't introduced you. Bryan, this is Sheriff Mac Riggs. Mac, this is my cousin, Bryan Elliott."

"Cousin?" Mac couldn't help blurting out. Stunned, he shook the hand Bryan had offered, still reeling with this new turn of events. Relief swamped him, and Mac took his first calm breath since the man had showed up on his doorstep.

"Yep. Bryan and I are cousins. And I have a whole family back in New York, Mac. A whole big crazy family. I can't wait to tell you all about them."

Mac ran his hand along his jaw, his lips pursed, listening to Jane—to Bridget Elliott—as she filled him in about her life. She'd smile as the memories washed over her, reciting them to him but at the same time seeming to relive them.

Mac cursed his bad luck. Bridget Elliott was a rich New York socialite, whose family had an estate in the Hamptons, no less. Her family owned one of the most prestigious magazine publishing houses in the world. Bridget was the photo editor for *Charisma,* a high-end fashion magazine that catered to the rich and beyond. Hell, he'd been sleeping with a woman who under any other circumstances he wouldn't have given the time of day. Bridget Elliott was way out of his league.

He'd already had one failed relationship with a woman who had higher aspirations than bedding down with a small-town sheriff. Mac couldn't help but place Bridget—he'd have to get used to calling her that—in the same category. Bridget Elliott might look like Jane Doe, might talk like Jane Doe, but Mac wouldn't deceive himself. They were worlds apart.

Bridget Elliott had money to burn.

Her family could probably buy the whole of Winchester without so much as blinking their eyes.

"Bryan owns this very trendy restaurant called Un Nuit. His place is great. I can't wait for you to see it, Mac."

Mac held himself in check. "Bridget," he said awkwardly, using her real name for the first time. "Your cousin Bryan might own a restaurant, but there's more to him than meets the eye."

"What do you mean?"

"Your family is powerful and wealthy, yet they couldn't find you. But Bryan did. And he wouldn't speak of his methods. Take it from a man in law enforcement, your cousin isn't exactly who he seems."

"Oh, don't be silly, Mac. Of course he is. Bryan just likes to be...cryptic at times."

Mac nodded. "That's one way to describe him."

But Bridget was eager to go on. "And guess what, Mac. The boots. I know why you couldn't track them down in Italy. Poor little Carmello DiVincenza, a genius at shoemaking, died two years ago. My boots were the very last ones he'd made. No wonder I cherish them. He lived and worked and died in this little village just south of Florence called Micello. I remember doing a photo shoot there for a story with *Charisma*. He insisted on creating the boots especially for me."

"So you trot around the world, doing whatever you do for this magazine." Mac leaned back on the sofa, glad that they were alone. Lizzie was still out with Lyle, and Bryan had left a few minutes ago, to give Bridget time to collect her thoughts. Of course, he wouldn't say where he was staying. He'd just used the classic Arnold Schwarzenegger line: "I'll be back."

"No, not always. I work in the offices at EPH—that's Elliott Publication Holdings—but on occasion, I go on location for a shoot. I love Europe, and Italy is my favorite country."

"So you're the one with Trump money." Mac couldn't keep the edge out of his voice. Bridget couldn't help who she was, but he didn't have to like it.

She stared at him. "Mac. I know what you're thinking, but I'm not a spoiled little rich girl. In fact, I deplore everything my family stands for. It's the reason I came to Winchester to begin with. My family is full of secrets."

"What family doesn't have its secrets?"

"Oh, but my family is different. We have a whole

volume of secrets. And I plan to expose them all—and expose my grandfather for the man he truly is. There'll be no whitewashing my accounting of his life. I'm writing a revealing book to expose his self-serving manipulations. My book will uncover truths that have been secret for decades."

Mac shook his head, staring at Bridget, seeing her with clear eyes. She wasn't his Jane Doe anymore. She was a cynical woman bent on…what? Revenge? Payback? Or did she feel that her tell-all book would somehow be justified?

"Sounds like you're going to hurt a whole lot of people."

"To clear the air, Mac. Patrick Elliott, my esteemed grandfather, has gotten away with too much to get to the top. He's got the media in his back pocket. All these years he's covered his tracks well. He needs to be stopped. He's only getting what he deserves."

"And you think a book is going to solve all the problems?" Mac rose. He set his hands on his hips, staring down at her. "Innocent people will get hurt."

"But innocent people *have* been hurt, Mac. I came here because I received an anonymous tip that my aunt Finola's child might be living right here in Winchester. A child my grandfather forced her to give up for adoption when she was just fifteen years old. He'd used his power and influence over her and it nearly destroyed her. *Charisma* is all the life she has now. It's not fair, Mac. She shouldn't have to go through life not knowing her daughter. I came here to find her. I know she was adopted by a couple living here in Winchester."

"That's what brought you here?"

She nodded, standing to face him. "It's the sole reason. I came here to find and reunite Aunt Fin with her daughter."

"It's none of your business, Bridget." Mac still couldn't get used to her real name. It sounded false on his lips, as though he wasn't speaking with the same woman who'd had come to mean everything to him. "It's not your battle."

"It is my battle. Fighting my grandfather and uncovering the truth about him is what I set out to do six months ago. The book is the means to the end. It'll put a stop to all the scandals. My family can then put the past behind them. Finding Aunt Fin's child will make her happy and will send a message to Grandfather Patrick that he can no longer mess with our lives. Aunt Fin has suffered for too many years. Her daughter would be twenty-three now."

That rang a bell with Mac. Could it be that it was his friend Travis's daughter whom Bridget was looking for? Jessie was the right age, twenty-three, and she'd been adopted as a baby from a teenaged mother. Travis didn't talk much about Jessie's adoption now, having fallen in love with his daughter from the moment he'd laid eyes on her. No one would guess that Jessie and Travis didn't hold a flesh-and-blood bond.

Mac and Travis went way back, and recently the rancher had been helping Mac fix up his ranch house.

Hell, the last thing his friend needed was to have his life turned upside down by Bridget's interference. It was bad enough that Travis lost his wife a few years back.

"You're messing with people's lives, Bridget." Mac stood firm, speaking adamantly. "Don't do this."

"I have to."

"No, you don't!" He turned his back on her and threw his arms up in disgust. "Of all the rotten luck. I can't believe I fell in love with a rich bitch, willing to destroy so many lives." Then he turned to her, hot anger reaching the boiling point. "You're not the woman I found up on Deerlick Canyon. Not if you do this. That woman isn't vindictive. She's not so cynical that she feels justified in damaging lives. Let it be, *Bridget*."

"I can't, Mac," she said, facing him squarely. "Don't you understand? The book is nearly finished. Finding Aunt Fin's child will be the final chapter."

Mac stared into those vivid, gleaming blue eyes. He realized he'd finally opened his heart to allow love inside, to have it all shatter around him in one quick instant. Bridget Elliott—bitter, cynical and so damn beautiful that she took his breath away—wasn't the woman for him. She'd been born with a silver spoon in her mouth and could be doing something positive with her life; instead she chose to cause misery and heartache to those around her.

Mac wouldn't allow her to cause that misery here, not now, not in his town and not in his house. He wouldn't do that to Travis or to himself. There was only one solution. "When your cousin returns, I think you should leave."

"Mac," she said in a quiet voice, tearing his heart out with her plea.

He held firm, but he had to force the next words. "If you intend to go ahead with your plans, you have no place here."

Slowly she nodded, and Mac cringed inwardly. She wouldn't give up. "I have to finish what I started."

"Then we'll have to say goodbye. Go back to New York, Bridget. It's where you belong."

Lizzie burst through the door, her face awash with joy. "Lyle asked me out on a date! And he offered to help when I move into my apartment. Jane, we have to shop. I need your help in finding the perfect outfit."

Mac took a last look at Jane, or the woman he wished was Jane, then directed his gaze to his sister. "She's not Jane. Her name is Bridget Elliott and she'll be on the next flight to New York."

"I can't thank you enough, Bridget. I couldn't have put together these outfits without your help. But with all that's on your mind, I can't believe you still wanted to help me shop," Lizzie said, plopping her shopping bags on Bridget's bed.

Bridget sat down on the bed and soon Lizzie joined her. "I made you a promise, Lizzie. Besides, you've done so much for me and I wanted to return the favor. It was fun. Took my mind off…things."

"Like the fact that your plane leaves in three hours? I can't help it. I wish you weren't leaving," Lizzie said with great sadness. "My brother needs you."

Bridget leaned back to rest her head against the pillow. She closed her eyes, and visions of Mac rushed forward. His rare smile, the way he would hold her, the tender way he made love to her. "Mac doesn't understand what I'm trying to do."

"No, and he probably won't change his mind, either. He's always been so sure of what's right."

Bridget snapped her eyes open. "So you don't think I'm doing the right thing, either?"

Lizzie took hold of her hand. "It's none of my business, really. It's between you and my brother." She squeezed her hand firmly. "I know Mac's hurting, too. He didn't say much, but it's all on his face, the pain of losing you. You have to promise me one thing, Bridget."

"Anything."

"Don't return a thing he's given you, not the clothes, not the jewelry. And for heaven's sake, don't you dare try to pay him back. I know my brother. That'll just about kill him."

Bridget nodded. "I'm glad you told me. But I want to do something to return your kindness."

"Just be my friend, Bridget. That's all I need. Maybe give me some fashion advice once in a while?"

Bridget chuckled. "Sure."

"I'm going to miss you."

Tears stung Bridget's eyes. She'd come to love both brother and sister in this household. And she knew that her life would never be the same since knowing them. She wrapped her arms around Lizzie and they hugged tightly.

"Me, too. But do yourself a favor, Lizzie. Don't back

down with Mac. Don't change your mind about moving out or your plans with Lyle."

Lizzie sat thoughtfully for a moment. "But my brother—"

"Lizzie," Bridget began firmly, "don't you dare. You've devoted your life to Mac. You've been a good sister, and I think Mac really does want your happiness. I'm hoping I got through to him, at least about that."

Lizzie smiled. "I hope so, too."

Bridget rose and began filling the duffel bag Lizzie had given her. Within a minute, she was all packed and ready.

Mac popped his head in the doorway. "Your cousin's here to pick you up."

"Oh." It all seemed to be happening so fast. Bridget turned to stare into Lizzie's pretty brown eyes. "I have to go."

Lizzie nodded and stood. "I know."

"Bye, my friend." Bridget held back the flood of tears surging forth. Crying wouldn't help the situation. What was done was done, and Bridget knew her time in Winchester was over.

"Goodbye," Lizzie whispered, giving her one last hug. "I'll entertain Bryan while you two say goodbye."

Lizzie left and Bridget stared into Mac's dark eyes. She grabbed the straps of the duffel bag, which was filled with things that would be a constant reminder of Winchester County and Mac Riggs. Things that held special meaning…things she couldn't part with. "I guess it's goodbye, then."

Strong and tall and always in control, Mac nodded,

keeping silent. Bridget walked over to him. "I can't leave without thanking you for everything, Mac," she said softly, drinking in the sight of him. She hoped she'd never forget those intense dark eyes, the way the tic worked in his jaw when he thought about something too long, or the way his eyes softened on her when they made love. "You're an excellent lawman and a wonderful man."

With that, Bridget reached up to kiss his cheek, giving him a soft, subtle peck that belied her true feelings. But Mac didn't want her to kiss him. He didn't want her in his life or in his house. She'd been effectively tossed out. Not even his admission of love earlier helped this moment, since his next words, "rich bitch," had cut deep into her heart. He didn't want to love her. And that hurt the most, because Bridget loved him with everything she had inside. She loved him no matter what. But their differences had torn them apart.

"I'm going to miss Winchester," she said honestly. "And you most of all."

She strode past him, hoping he'd call her back. Hoping he'd say something. Silence ensued. And his indifference said it all.

"You ready, cuz?" Bryan asked, grabbing her duffel bag and opening the front door.

She stopped and turned around, looking into Mac's cool dark eyes one last time. "I'm ready. Let's go home."

Eleven

"You okay?" Bryan asked as he drove along the private road leading to The Tides, Patrick Elliott's Hamptons estate. Bridget peered out the car window, noting the manicured gardens, the long circular driveway leading up to the estate and the house itself, understated yet so grand. Salty sea air from the Atlantic just below the bluff brought back memories of happier times, when she would run and play in the sand along the beach with her brothers and cousins.

Bridget remembered it all. The familiarity didn't bring her comfort, though. Her mind and heart were still fixed on a cozy Colorado house and a small-town sheriff who had embedded himself in her soul. "I will be, once

I see Mom. You said she was okay, right? It's been two weeks since I've seen her."

Bryan nodded. "She's been worried about you, Bridget."

"I'm so sorry about that." Bridget hated to worry her mother, but she hadn't planned on losing her memory. She hadn't planned on falling in love, either. Even now, as she thought back on her time with Mac, she couldn't honestly say that she'd change anything. Knowing him and loving him had brought a greater wealth to her life than anything her grandfather might fathom. But Mac couldn't understand why Bridget had to change things in her family.

"Mom's got enough to deal with right now." Four months ago Karen Elliott had undergone a double mastectomy. Ever since then she'd spent a lot of time at her in-laws' Hamptons estate.

"She's a tough cookie. Never lets on when she's down. But I know she'll be thrilled to see you."

Bryan stopped the car just outside the front doors. "I can't come in. I've got pressing business. Give Aunt Karen my love, will you?"

"I sure will. And that 'pressing business' has to do with the restaurant, right, cuz?"

Bryan slanted her a look. "What else?"

"Right," Bridget said, slanting him a look right back. She wondered if Mac's instincts were right about Bryan. Could her cousin be more than he appeared?

Bridget exited the car, giving him a big hug when he came around to her side to hand her the duffel bag.

"Thanks again for finding me. I don't know when or how I might have gotten my memory back without you."

Bryan kissed her cheek. "All in a day's work," he said. Right before hopping back into the driver's seat, he added, "For a second or two back in Colorado, I wondered if you really wanted your memory back."

"Another story for another day, Bryan." She waved in farewell, watching him leave, before climbing the steps to her grandfather's home. And when she opened the door, the scent of grandeur filled the air, from the lavish Italian marble beneath her feet to the rich antiques lining the wall of the regal foyer.

Always understated. Always elegant. Her grandmom Maeve had decorated the estate in the same manner that she'd carried herself.

Minutes later, Bridget found her mother sitting peacefully in the solarium, looking out at the ocean. The water took on a soft glow as the sunlight began to fade. Bridget watched her for a long moment before announcing herself, noting her pale complexion, a sign that the chemotherapy was sapping her strength. The colorful satin scarf around her head was just another reminder of what her mother had gone through recently.

"Hi, Mom."

Her mother turned at the sound of her voice. "Bridget, honey." She stood and her smile lit her face with renewed energy. Bridget ran into her mother's warm and loving arms. "I'm so glad you're all right. Any complications from the fall or the amnesia?"

She shook her head, breathing in her mother's

familiar flowery scent. "No, nothing. I'm fine, but I've been worried about you."

"I'm recuperating. It's a slow process, but I'm going to be okay."

The embrace lasted a long time, Bridget finding it hard to let her mother go. When they finally broke apart to take their seats facing the incredible Atlantic waves, Bridget spilled her heart to her mother about her time in Winchester with Mac and her confusion about writing her book.

Karen Elliott gave her a good piece of advice. "There's only one person who knows what's right for you, honey."

"I've set out to do something, Mom. I've never been a quitter."

Her mother smiled warmly, her green eyes bright and honest. "Sometimes we get exactly what we want, only to find out it's not what we wanted at all. Take some time, honey. Think what's most important to you."

"That's all I have been thinking about since leaving Colorado."

"Well, then, let me give you something else to think about. Your father and I are going to be grandparents. Gannon and Erika have just announced that they are expecting a baby."

"Really? Oh, Mom, that's great news."

"Yes, and I plan on being healthy enough to babysit my new grandchild."

"You will be, Mom." Bridget sighed, thinking about her one time jet-setting brother. "Just think, my big brother is going to be a father."

Karen chuckled. "Hard to believe, but yes. I think he finally met his match with Erika. They're very happy."

"Well, I'm happy for them."

Her mother reached for her hands, taking them in hers and applying gentle pressure. "That's all I want for my children, honey. Happiness. Sometimes it's not that hard to find, if you look in the right place."

Bridget's loft in SoHo was spacious and stylish but certainly didn't offer the same type of elegance her grandparents' home in the Hamptons did. She smiled as she roamed around, surrounded by furnishings and artwork that depicted her personality. Casual, contemporary and all the things a young twenty-eight-year-old woman might enjoy. But as she'd driven home this morning down Broadway, after spending the night at The Tides, she realized she'd never considered how cluttered the avenues were, how busy, the streets lined with shops, restaurants and brick buildings that looked as though they'd been here from the beginning of time.

All familiar.

Yet nothing so far had seemed quite right.

She would simply have to readjust. After her ordeal in Colorado, she supposed it was natural to feel a little "off" and out of tune with her normal way of life.

Bridget clicked on the radio and turned the dial, finding the station she wanted, tapping her toes to the music, killing time until her visitor arrived. When the knock came Bridget sighed with relief and strode quickly to the door, unlocking and sliding the heavy panel open.

"I brought wedding pictures," her new cousin Misty announced, lifting a white photo album in the air.

Bridget glanced at Misty's five-months-pregnant belly. In two weeks it seemed as though she'd grown another dress size, but Bridget wouldn't dare share those thoughts with her. Misty looked happy and pregnant pretty.

"Misty, I'm so glad you came to visit. Come in. Did you get your pictures back already?"

"Just the proofs. We'll get to that later." Misty gave her a good looking over, and once she seemed satisfied, she said, "You had us all worried sick. My maid of honor disappears right after our wedding reception and no one knows a thing! You didn't tell a soul where you were going. It's a good thing Bryan knew how to find you."

"My mistake. I'll never do anything like that again. Next time I'll be sure to let someone know where I'm heading."

Misty's eyes grew wide and her expression left no room for doubt that she didn't approve. "Next time?"

Bridget couldn't hold back a laugh. "Sit down. Take a load off."

"Hey, watch it. I'm older than you, but I still have some moves."

Both sat down on Bridget's cream leather sofa in an area of the loft known as the great room. Three rooms collided into each other and this one was where she relaxed, read, watched television or simply stared out of the giant floor-to-ceiling windows to the street below.

"I thought you used up all your moves on Cullen."

Her belly rolled when she chuckled. "Bridget, thank God you're home."

"Yeah," she said quietly, biting her lip. "I'm home."

"Uh-oh, I know that look. What's wrong?"

Bridget lifted her shoulders, shrugging casually, but inside she felt weighted down by heartache and indecision. "Nothing much, really. Except that I fell in love with the man who probably saved my life. He took me in when I had nowhere to go. Sheriff Mac Riggs. He thinks I'm a spoiled rich socialite with nothing better to do than to cause trouble. He doesn't approve of what I'm trying to do."

"Oh, I see." Misty's green eyes positively gleamed. "Mmm, a sheriff, you say? Tall, handsome? I bet he looks real good in his uniform."

The recollection of Mac in his uniform and *out* of his uniform was never far from her mind. "You're not making this any easier."

"Then let me ask you this—if he's so awful, why bother?"

"Yeah, you're right. Why bother? He is awful. Awfully stubborn. Awfully demanding." And then she softened her voice to a mere whisper. "Awfully kind. Awfully generous. Awfully sexy. So awfully good-looking that my heart stopped every time he walked into the room."

"Wow," Misty said, with a shake of her head. "So what are you waiting for? You're obviously crazy about him. Go back to Colorado and change his mind about you."

Bridget stood up and walked over to the window, glancing down at the street below. Traffic had come to a halt where two drivers had collided in a fender bender. They faced each other on the street, eyes bulging, mouths flapping and fingers pointing. She could only guess at the kind of language they used. She turned back to Misty. "I don't think I can change his mind."

"For a time Cullen didn't think he could change my mind, either, but he did. I wasn't making it easy on him. Thank goodness I put aside my misgivings. We're very happy," she said, patting her growing belly, "with a little one on the way. Bridget, if it's even remotely possible for you to have that kind of happiness, then do whatever it takes to make it happen."

Bridget took a deep, steadying breath, absorbing Misty's advice. But she still had doubts. She'd made herself a promise to write the book that would expose Patrick Elliott. And what of her aunt Fin? Didn't she deserve some happiness, too? "I'm still not sure, Misty. But I'll think about it."

"Don't think too long, my friend. Sounds like this guy has hunk-eligibility status." She fell silent for a moment as the radio blasted out Gretchen Wilson singing about rednecked women. "Heck, this guy's got you listening to country music. That *has* to mean something, honey. Now, I didn't just come over here to check on you. You're the photo editor in the family. How about taking a look at my proofs? I need help picking out a hundred or so for our wedding album."

"Gee, Misty, only a hundred?" she said on a teasing note, happy to have something productive to do today.

Tomorrow, she planned to start back to work at *Charisma*.

Bridget walked the halls of *Charisma* as she'd done a thousand times before, greeted by her employees and co-workers with welcoming smiles and hellos. She stopped to speak with a few, briefly explaining about her absence in the simplest terms. The trip to Colorado and her bout of amnesia were still too raw, too personal to talk about in detail, other than to the very few people she truly trusted.

Aunt Fin fell into that category. Bridget had worked alongside her for years and during that time they'd formed a close bond. Aunt Fin babied *Charisma* as if it were her own child. Everyone knew it. Everyone understood the need behind the countless hours and the devotion she put into the magazine. There was a void in her aunt's life, and Bridget had hoped to remedy that by finding the daughter taken from her at birth.

"Morning," she said, popping her head in the doorway of Finola's office.

Aunt Fin, knee-deep in paperwork as usual, slowly lifted her head, taking her eyes off the layout she'd been studying on her desk. "Bridget!"

She stood and came around her desk, meeting Bridget halfway into the room. Aunt Fin wrapped her arms around her, giving her a big hug, then pulled back to look into her eyes. "Thank God. You look wonderful."

"I do?" Bridget hadn't gotten much sleep last night. Or the night before. Pale and weary, she hadn't spent too much time covering up with makeup, either, this morning. But Aunt Fin always had something nice to say to her.

"You do to me, Bridget. I was worried sick about you." She guided her to the comfy sofa her aunt often used as a makeshift bed when working through the night. "Have a seat and tell me all about it."

"Don't we have a deadline?"

"We do. It can wait. Besides, we're ahead of schedule right now. I want to hear it all."

Bridget sat down with her aunt and held nothing back. She told Aunt Fin everything, from the anonymous tip about Finola's child she'd received at Cullen and Misty's wedding to her falling in love with and eventual breaking up with Mac. Her aunt sat back and listened attentively, and when Bridget had finally had her say, Aunt Fin took hold of her hands.

"You're my niece, Bridget. You know that I love you dearly, but I can't have you ruining your life for me. I want to know my daughter. I've dreamed of it often, but I don't want to cause a disruption in her life. I realize that she might not want to know me, but if she does, I've managed to list myself in a worldwide database. All of my information is out there on an adoption Web site. I'm easy to find, if my daughter feels the need. I only hope and pray that she's had a good life. And when the time is right, we'll find each other. So, write that book if you absolutely must, but I'd advise not doing it, Bridget. It won't change anything. If you immerse yourself in anger and resentment, you'll lose something more important. Love. And nothing is more precious than that. Not a bestselling book. Not even a bestselling magazine," she said with a sad smile.

"But—"

"No buts, Bridget. My father did something that ruined my life, but don't let him ruin yours. Scandalizing Patrick Elliott won't give you a moment of satisfaction, and he'll still end up the winner, while you…you'll have lost the man you love. Is it worth the price?"

Bridget drew her lip in, contemplating. "I hadn't quite thought of it in those terms."

"How much is Mac's love worth to you, Bridget? If you can let go of the past, you could have a wonderful future."

"That's a big if."

"Well, I'll give you another if. If it were me, I'd be on the next jet back to Colorado."

Bridget took Aunt Fin's advice and the next jet back to Colorado. She stood outside the Winchester County Sheriff's Station, butterflies attacking her stomach, her heart pounding madly and her head spinning. It was nearly midnight and she'd learned from Lizzie that Mac had been putting in late hours at the station these days. Mac's sister had seemed surprised to see her on her doorstep at that late hour, but she hadn't flinched, merely told her where she could find Mac, giving her a nod of reassurance and a big hug.

Bridget had needed that extra bit of encouragement. She'd always met her battles head-on, but this time it was different. This time her future was at stake. She was taking a giant leap of faith here.

Bridget entered the station house and was greeted by a deputy sheriff who recognized her. "He's in his office. Maybe you could do something to put a smile on his face. He's crankier than my old water heater."

Bridget nearly lost her nerve, but she talked herself out of fleeing the scene. She had to play this out. If she didn't, then she'd never know whether she stood a chance with the only man she'd ever love. She took the steps necessary to reach his office door, and knocked softly.

"What?" he bellowed.

His bluster made her smile. He didn't scare her. He never had. Instead, the sound of his gruff voice reminded her of how much she loved him.

She opened his door and stepped inside. "Working kind of late, aren't you?"

Mac snapped his head up from his desk. Surprise registered on his face, and his eyes were unreadable, except for one quick flash of hope. Then, catching himself, he looked down at the papers he'd been working on. "If you're here about your aunt's child, I think I know how you might find her."

"No, that's not why I'm here, Mac. Aunt Fin doesn't need or want my help. I've given up that search. She's listed her name on an adoption database. If her daughter wants to find her, she can."

Mac pursed his lips and nodded, keeping his eyes downcast. "We found your rental car in the lake about a mile up from where the others were found. Found the boys responsible, too."

"That's good, Mac. I knew you'd find them."

"Your luggage wasn't in there. They'd disposed of it."

"It doesn't matter."

Mac lifted his eyes to hers finally, staring at her, then he shifted his gaze to her throat. Bridget fingered the silver necklace he'd given her, the necklace she had never removed.

"No, I suppose it wouldn't. So why are you here?"

Bridget smiled and walked over to the side of his desk. Mac leaned way back in his chair, putting space between them. He couldn't let his guard down. Not yet. Not until he knew why she'd come. She looked beautiful and elegant, even though she wore a pair of blue jeans. They weren't Levi's, but some designer label that probably cost five times more than they should. Over them she wore the T-shirt he'd once given her. She'd rolled up the sleeves and tied the shirt at her waist, the initials WCSD crossing over her breasts. Winchester County Sheriff's Department.

Ah, hell.

Bridget dug deep into her big black tote and came up with a white bag from Colorado Chuck's. "One for me and one for you," she said, setting two Pike's Peak burgers out in front of him. The sloppy chili and onion-filled burgers stunk up the place, but Mac didn't give a damn. A smile lifted the corners of his mouth.

"Aside from a good meal, I came here to file a missing person's report. Seems that Bridget Elliott is missing." She seated herself on top of Mac's desk and leaned in a bit. Mac breathed in her scent, gazed at her silky blond hair and looked into her big lavender-blue eyes.

"Is she?"

"Well, the cynical and ruthless part of her is missing. And I'm sure that part of her will never be found again. Gone for good."

"And what else should I put in this report?"

"Well, it seems that Bridget Elliott still wants to write a book."

Mac's eyebrows arched up and he cursed the hope he'd experienced the second she walked into his office. She hadn't changed. She still meant to write that mean-spirited book.

"A children's book. Seems Bridget loved reading to the little ones at the bookstore. She thinks she might have found her true calling, writing children's books. That's *all* she plans on writing, Mac." Bridget smiled and her eyes shone with light. "Jane and Bridget are one and the same. I can't deny who I am. Yes, I'm wealthy, and all my life I've had privileges most people don't dare to imagine. But I've changed, Mac. Living here with you opened my eyes and my heart to something more important. The only thing I want now is your love, if you'll have me."

Hope sprung up again at her admission. She'd given up her idea of writing that scandalous book about her family. Maybe she was more like his Jane Doe than she thought.

Mac rose from his seat and stood before her. He braced both hands on the desk, trapping her so close that only inches separated their bodies. "Are you saying you're willing to give up trips to Europe, designer clothes and a lifestyle that most women only dream about?"

Bridget wrapped both arms around his neck and nodded. "For a chance at a lifetime of Pike's Peak burgers, rides out at your ranch on Daisy Mae and waking up with you every morning, Sheriff Riggs? You bet."

Mac could hardly believe he'd heard right. Heart pounding, head ringing, he had to ask, "Are you sure?"

Bridget's smile faded and for a moment he thought he'd imagined it all. "Mac, my whole family's in New York. I love them. I'll need to be in New York sometimes."

"We can manage that."

"We can?" she said, a hopeful note in her voice.

"Hell, Bridget. Look at this." He opened his desk drawer and lifted out the ticket he had tucked away. He handed it to her.

"It's a ticket to New York," she said, slightly puzzled. Then her beautiful eyes flashed brightly. "You were coming to see me tomorrow?"

"Planning on making a fool out of myself. I'd hoped to talk some sense into you and bring you home."

Joy washed over Bridget's face and those twin dimples peeked out, deep and adorable. Mac had never known love this powerful before. He'd never known that he could love someone so different from himself. He and Bridget came from opposite worlds, yet here he was, so deeply in love that he'd set aside all his misgivings and doubts to take the greatest leap of faith he'd ever had to face. "I'm crazy about you, sweetheart."

Bridget tossed her head back, her eyes shining. "I'm crazy about you, too."

Mac dipped into his desk drawer one more time, coming up with a black velvet box. Bridget gasped when she noticed it.

"Well, I might as well make a fool of myself tonight," he muttered. "Bridget Elliott, I love you with all of my heart. Will you—"

Bridget grabbed the black box and opened it. "Yes, yes! Oh, it's beautiful, Mac. My answer is yes."

He chuckled and placed the diamond ring on her finger. "Marry me," he finished, but he already had his answer. "Be my wife."

"Oh, Mac. I love you so much," she breathed quietly, as much in awe as he was.

He bent and kissed his soon-to-be wife deeply, his heart filled with love and devotion. The kiss went longer and deeper than Mac had expected, their mouths and bodies hungry for each other. When Bridget leaned back on his desk, papers flew as Mac followed her down.

"Mac," she whispered in a raspy voice, "you think it's a crime to make love to the sheriff in his office?"

Mac lifted himself off of her. "Probably," he said, walking swiftly to his office door and locking it good and tight before returning to the desk. He covered her body with his and claimed her lips in a long, slow, sexy kiss.

"But it'd be more than a crime if we didn't, sweetheart. It'd be a damn shame."

* * * * *

THE ELLIOTTS *saga continues with*
Kara Lennox's UNDER DEEPEST COVER,
available this July from Silhouette Desire.

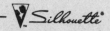

SPECIAL EDITION™

Welcome to Danbury Way— where nothing is as it seems...

Megan Schumacher has managed to maintain a low profile on Danbury Way by keeping the huge success of her graphics business a secret. But when a new client turns out to be a neighbor's sexy ex-husband, rumors of their developing romance quickly start to swirl.

THE RELUCTANT CINDERELLA

by CHRISTINE RIMMER

Available July 2006

Don't miss the first book from the Talk of the Neighborhood miniseries.

Silhouette
BOMBSHELL

The Marian priestesses were destroyed long ago,
but their daughters live on. The time has come
for the heiresses to learn of their legacy, to unite
the pieces of a powerful mosaic and bring light to
a secret their ancestors died to protect.

The Madonna Key

Follow their quests each month.

Lost Calling by Evelyn Vaughn,
July 2006

Haunted Echoes by Cindy Dees,
August 2006

Dark Revelations by Lorna Tedder,
September 2006

Shadow Lines by Carol Stephenson,
October 2006

Hidden Sanctuary by Sharron McClellan,
November 2006

Veiled Legacy by Jenna Mills,
December 2006

Seventh Key by Evelyn Vaughn,
January 2007

**Hidden in the secrets of antiquity,
lies the unimagined truth...**

Introducing

ROGUE ANGEL™

a brand-new line filled with mystery
and suspense, action and adventure,
and a fascinating look into history.

And it all begins with DESTINY.

In a sealed crypt in
France, where the
terrifying legend of
the beast of Gevaudan
begins to unravel,
Annja Creed discovers
a stunning artifact
that will seal her destiny.

*Available every other
month starting
July 2006, wherever
you buy books.*

GOLD
EAGLE®

HARLEQUIN®

Super Romance

THE PRODIGAL'S RETURN

by Anna DeStefano

Prom night for Jenn Gardner and Neal Cain turned
into a tragedy that tore them apart. Eight years
later, Jenn made a life for herself and her young
daughter. But when Neal comes home, Jenn sees that
he is still consumed with the past. Maybe she can
convince him that he's paid enough and deserves
happiness a second time around.

"Anna DeStefano's remarkable stories of the healing
power of love touch the heart with hope. One of the
genre's rising stars..."
—Gayle Wilson, two-time
RITA® Award-winning author

On sale July 2006!
*Available wherever books are sold, including most
bookstores, supermarkets, discount stores and drugstores.*

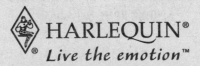

HARLEQUIN®
Live the emotion™

COMING NEXT MONTH